carter house girls

D0027013

HOMECOMING QUEEN

MELODY CARLSON

DISCARD

ZONDERVAN®

ZONDERVAN.com/
AUTHORTRACKER
follow your favorite authors

ZONDERVAN

Homecoming Queen
Copyright © 2008 by Melody Carlson

www.zondervan.com

Requests for information should be addressed to:
Zondervan, *Grand Rapids, Michigan 49530*

Library of Congress Cataloging-in-Publication Data

Carlson, Melody.
      Homecoming queen / by Melody Carlson.
        p. cm. -- (Carter House girls ; bk. 3)
      Summary: At the Carter boardinghouse for rich teenaged girls who are interested
in fashion, the race for high school homecoming queen turns friends and roommates
against one another, and, as the votes roll in, some of the girls grow smarter and
closer to God, while others seem to make the same mistakes over again.
      ISBN 978-0-310-71490-3 (softcover)
      [1. Boardinghouses--Fiction. 2. Interpersonal relations--Fiction. 3. Conduct of life--
Fiction. 4. Christian life--Fiction. 5. High schools--Fiction. 6. Schools--Fiction.] I. Title.
      PZ7.C216637Ho 2008
      [Fic]--dc22

                                                  2008016871

Internet addresses (websites, blogs, etc.) and telephone numbers printed in this book are
offered as a resource to you. These are not intended in any way to be or imply an endorse-
ment on the part of Zondervan, nor do we vouch for the content of these sites and numbers for the life of this book.

Zonderkidz is a trademark of Zondervan

Interior design by Christine Orejuela-Winkelman

Printed in the United States of America

09 10 11 12 13 14 • 24 23 22 21 20 19 18 17 16 15 14 13 12 11 10 9 8 7 6 5 4 3

Homecoming Queen

1

homecoming queen

DJ Lane jumped at the sound of someone opening her bedroom door. It was well past midnight, and the house had been quiet for at least an hour now. The floor creaked as the intruder slipped into the room. With a pounding heart, DJ wondered if she should scream for help or simply play dead. Without daring to breathe, she peeked over the edge of her comforter just in time to see her long-lost roommate quietly closing the door.

"Taylor!" cried DJ as she threw back the covers and leaped out of bed. "Where on earth have you been?" Taylor had been AWOL for several days, and everyone in the house — including Taylor's enemies — had been frantic with worry.

"Shh!" Taylor held a finger to her lips and then shirked off her leather jacket. It appeared to be soaking wet, and she dropped it to the floor with a heavy thud. "Don't wake up the whole house."

"We *should* wake them." DJ turned on a bedside lamp and stared at her runaway friend. Taylor, usually stunningly beautiful with her perfect olive-toned complexion, exotic eyes, and luxurious dark curls, now looked like a train wreck. Plus, she was dripping wet. "I mean, everyone's been freaking over you, Taylor. We should tell my grandmother that you're back and—"

"Tomorrow," said Taylor as she unzipped her jeans and peeled them off. "It's late now. I just want to grab a hot shower and go to bed. No fuss."

"But what about the police and the—"

"Seriously DJ, I am dead tired." Taylor scowled as she tossed the soggy jeans next to the jacket on the floor. "We'll sort it out tomorrow. I promise."

"But the others will be so relieved to—"

"I *mean* it, DJ," hissed Taylor. "Shut up and go back to sleep!" Then, acting like *no big deal*—as if everyone in the entire town hadn't been freaking over her disappearance—Taylor slipped into the bathroom and quietly but firmly shut the door.

DJ felt slightly enraged. Wide awake and full of questions, she wanted to go in there and confront her roommate. She wanted to demand answers and explanations for this crazy missing act that had put everyone in Carter House on high alert this week. Who did Taylor think she was anyway?

DJ could hear the water in the shower running and, re-membering that tomorrow was a school day, got back into her bed. As aggravating as it was to have Taylor pull a stunt like this, sneaking back into the house while everyone was sleep-ing, it probably did make more sense to sort this whole thing out by the light of day. And despite feeling seriously irritated at Taylor's nonchalance, DJ was also hugely relieved that the girl was back.

DJ remembered the past couple of evenings and how she and the other Carter House girls had gathered and actually prayed—each in her own way—that Taylor would make it back safely. And now, just like that, Taylor was here—and it

8

seemed that she was just fine. Well, other than looking like a mess. Knowing Taylor, she would remedy this by morning. Still, DJ was curious as to where Taylor had been hiding out and even more curious about why she'd come back. Whatever the case, it did seem that God really had answered their prayers. Taylor was safe!

"You're kidding?" said Rhiannon. DJ had slipped into Rhiannon and Casey's room to share the news the following morning. "Taylor's back? Is she here right now?"

"Yep." DJ nodded as she sat down on Casey's bed, watching as Rhiannon quickly braided her long red curls to get them away from her face. She still had on pajamas, and DJ knew she'd awakened her, but she had to talk to someone. "Taylor got in late last night and she's still asleep. Where's Casey?"

"In the bathroom." Rhiannon shoved her feet into her slippers and yawned. "Did Taylor say where she'd been?"

"No. But she was soaking wet when she came in, so I can only assume she rode home on her Vespa."

"Yeah. It was pouring down last night."

Just then Casey emerged from the bathroom, wrapped in a towel. Her short wet hair stuck out in all directions. She stared curiously at DJ. "What's up?"

"Taylor's back."

Casey's already large brown eyes grew huge now. "She's *back?*"

"Yep." DJ quickly filled her in on the late-night arrival.

"And she's okay?" Casey's already pale complexion looked even paler now.

"As far as I can see. She's asleep right now."

"Did you tell her ... about me? I mean, that I'm the one who did the MySpace thing?"

"No. She wouldn't even let me talk to her."

Casey sank into the window seat cushion and slowly shook her head. "I guess this is when the stuff hits the fan, huh?"

"I don't know." DJ glanced nervously at Rhiannon, hoping she could say something encouraging.

"It's going to be okay," Rhiannon said to Casey in a soothing tone.

"How can you say that?" Casey looked at Rhiannon and then DJ. "I committed a crime! Libel!" It was true. Casey had posted some pretty nasty photos of Taylor on the Internet. Some shots had actually been "authentic," but others had been tampered with by Casey. She'd managed to create some very crude and lewd images that even Taylor had been unable to live down once they'd hit cyberspace.

"No one is prosecuting you," said DJ.

"Not yet. But that could all change today." Tears slid down Casey's cheeks. "I can't believe I was so stupid."

"None of us can believe it," said DJ.

"It seemed like a great idea at the time," said Casey, wiping her nose on the edge of her oversized towel. "I thought I was being so clever—getting even with Taylor. She deserved it after how she hurt Rhiannon."

"Revenge never works," said Rhiannon.

"Tell me about it." Casey sighed.

"And worrying about it won't change anything," said DJ.

"That's easy for you to say." Casey stood. "I'm the one who could end up in jail."

"You're a minor," said Rhiannon.

"Okay, juvenile detention." Casey tightly shut her eyes. "That's even worse."

"That would only happen if Taylor presses charges," said DJ. "Remember what Detective Howard told us the other day?"

"Of course she'll press charges," declared Casey hotly. "She's probably already spoken to a lawyer. I'm toast."

"You don't know that," said DJ.

"I need to get dressed," said Casey quickly, heading back to the bathroom. "If I'm going down, at least I can have some clothes on."

"You're not going down, Casey." DJ made an attempt at a laugh, but she knew it sounded fake.

After Casey returned to the bathroom, Rhiannon looked at DJ. "Do you think she'll really have to go into juvenile detention?"

DJ shrugged. "It seems crazy, but I suppose it's possible. According to Detective Howard, she did break the law. Taylor has the right to press charges."

"We really need to pray about this."

DJ nodded. "Yeah." She put her hand on the door handle and looked sympathetically toward the bathroom. "Well, I need to get ready for school. And I need to tell Grandmother what's up so she can notify the police."

"What about Taylor's parents? Do they know?"

DJ shrugged. "Guess that's Taylor's business."

DJ felt a mixture of emotions as she returned to her room. On one hand, she was relieved that Taylor was back—and safe. On the other hand, life would probably get complicated again. Casey was right, the stuff would be hitting the fan soon—and just after Casey had finally made an effort to fit in here at Carter House and after DJ's grandmother had decided not to send her home after all. All that could change now.

As DJ finished getting ready for school, she prayed for Casey. She wasn't even sure how to pray, so finally she just asked God to bring something good out of this mess. She had no idea what that might be, but she felt certain that God could do it.

"You done in there yet?" asked Taylor in a groggy voice.

"Sure," said DJ as she opened the bathroom door more fully. "I didn't know if you'd even be up yet. Are you planning on going to school today?"

Taylor shrugged then pushed a dark strand of curly hair out of her eyes. Even after her late night, and possibly riding her Vespa in the pouring rain, she still looked gorgeous. "I don't know."

"I'm going to let my grandmother know that you're back."

Taylor rolled her eyes. "Yeah. Whatever."

DJ controlled herself from saying something sarcastic back at her—like "Thank you very much, DJ. I appreciate your concern." She knew it wouldn't do anyone any good to get into a fight with Taylor today. If anything, she felt like she should be very placating, very kind and understanding. Maybe if she played her cards just right, she could induce a bit of Taylor's sympathy toward Casey. Possible, though unlikely.

"She's back, isn't she?" whispered Inez with dark, curious eyes. The housekeeper had stopped DJ on her way to Grandmother's room. "I saw her little green motorbike outside, and I know that means she's back."

DJ nodded. "Yes. She's back."

"Does this mean trouble, you think?"

"I don't know. Right now I just want to tell Grandmother."

"I'll tell Clara to set another place for breakfast."

"Thanks." Then DJ knocked on her grandmother's door. Although her bedroom was on the same floor as the girls, it was in the back of the house, with the stairway acting as a sort of buffer to the other rooms.

"Yes?" Grandmother opened the door, still wearing her rose-colored satin robe, as she peered blurrily at DJ. "What is it, Desiree?"

DJ quickly told her the news.

Grandmother blinked. "She's here now?"

"Yes."

"And she's all right?"

"She seems perfectly fine."

"Did she inform her parents?"

"I don't know. We haven't really had a chance to talk. I just wanted to let you know so you could contact the police and stuff."

"Yes. Yes, I'll get right to it." Grandmother smiled as she clasped her hands in front of her. "Oh, I'm so glad that she's back."

DJ nodded, but felt unsure.

"She's such a *beautiful* girl," said Grandmother.

DJ wondered what that really had to do with anything. "Well, yeah."

"And I have such plans for her."

"Oh." DJ got it. The old grooming-the-girls-to-be-models idea was poking up its ugly head again.

Grandmother put a thin, wrinkled hand on the side of DJ's face. "Oh, it's not that you're not pretty too, Desiree. You most certainly are. But that Taylor—" The old woman smacked her lips like she were about to devour a piece of chocolate cream pie—or more likely a carrot, knowing her. "That Taylor—well, she has the makings of a real supermodel."

"Right." DJ stepped away now. "So, you will let the police and everyone know?"

"Oh, yes, of course." Grandmother nodded in a vague kind of way that suggested that she had already forgotten about

13

Detective Howard and Taylor's parents, as if she had simply dismissed all of that as insignificant compared to the fact that Taylor had the "right stuff" to be molded into some kind of supermodel. Talk about delusional.

"And, Desiree," said Grandmother as DJ started to leave. "Please, tell Taylor that I'd like to see her in my room—before breakfast."

"Okay." DJ sighed.

"And don't slouch, dear," said Grandmother. Then she stood a bit taller herself, as if to show DJ how it was done. She held her pointed chin higher as she used the back of her fingers to give it a pat underneath, as if that might help the slightly sagging skin to tighten. "Good posture tells people that you believe in yourself, dear. It makes a good impression."

"Yeah, right." For her grandmother's sake, DJ stood a bit straighter, suppressing the urge to grind her teeth and growl as she walked back to her room. Sheesh. Sometimes DJ wondered if she was honestly related to that crazy old bat. DJ's mom, an intelligent and down to earth person, had been nothing like Grandmother. But then DJ's mom was dead. And DJ's dad didn't want to deal with a teenage daughter. Really, DJ knew she should be thankful for the old woman. But sometimes it was tough.

2

Homecoming Queen

"MY GRANDMOTHER WANTS TO SEE YOU," DJ informed Taylor. "Before breakfast, in her room."

"I'm almost done here," said Taylor as she applied some mascara to her already long, dark eyelashes. She blinked and looked at her reflection with what seemed a slightly critical frown that made no sense to DJ since the girl was obviously gorgeous.

"You look done to me," said DJ in a flat tone.

Taylor let out an exasperated sigh. "No offense, DJ, but you're not exactly the epitome of style."

"Thanks. I'll take that as a compliment."

Taylor turned from the mirror and seemed to study DJ. "I mean you've come a long way, but what is up with those shoes?"

DJ looked down at her old sneakers. "They're comfortable."

"Well, they look like you should give them back to the bag lady you stole them from."

"I wasn't planning on wearing them to school," said DJ defensively. "I just slipped them on for—"

15

"Never mind," snapped Taylor as she turned back to the mirror and picked up a large brush that she ran over hair, and then added some blush over her high cheekbones.

"So." DJ leaned against the bathroom door frame, watching. "Where were you anyway, Taylor? I mean, these past few days? Where were you hiding out?"

"Wouldn't you like to know?"

DJ shrugged. "Just curious."

"Well, if I told you I'd have to kill you."

DJ made a face. "Yeah, right. I'm sure you have some deep, dark secrets, don't you?"

"Don't we all?" Taylor put a layer of gloss over her already tinted lips then puckered up. "There," she said with satisfaction. "That's as good as it gets."

DJ stepped away from the door to let Taylor through, and both girls grabbed their bags. "So," said DJ, "you're really going to school today?"

Taylor kind of shrugged. "Yeah. Why not? I mean, I was thinking about Mr. Harper and the musical, and I want to make sure I get a role in it."

DJ tried not to look too shocked. And, really, why should she be? Just because Taylor had been slandered on MySpace, then turned into a missing person who had possibly been abducted or murdered—well, why should that change anything? In some ways, Taylor was a lot like Grandmother—it was all about appearances. As long as everyone looked good on the surface, well, who cared about what was underneath?

"I'm going to talk to Mrs. Carter now," said Taylor lightly. She slipped several silver bangle bracelets over a slender wrist. "See you at breakfast, sweetie." She made a little finger wave and then paused and actually tossed what seemed a fairly sincere smile at DJ. "And, I probably shouldn't tell you this, DJ, but you are the only person that I missed in this house."

DJ blinked. "Really?"

"Yeah, but don't let it go to your head."

"You can count on that."

Then Taylor breezed out of the room, leaving a trail of expensive Prada perfume behind her. DJ happened to know that the tiny bottle cost $125, which according to DJ's math estimates should run about ten bucks a squirt. Crazy.

DJ changed her shoes, did some quick tweaks to her makeup, and then hurried downstairs. She was eager to see Eliza and Kriti's reaction to the news that Taylor was back.

"Where is she?" asked Eliza before DJ was fully in the dining room.

"Talking to my grandmother."

"Did she tell you anything?" asked Kriti. "Like where she's been or—"

"Nope." DJ poured herself a cup of coffee and sat at the large formal table with the others. Everyone except Taylor and Grandmother were there. And all eyes were on DJ now.

"But she was okay?" asked Kriti with concerned eyes. "She wasn't kidnapped or anything?"

"I seriously doubt that." DJ dipped her spoon into the crystal sugar bowl and then dumped it into her coffee.

"I'm sure some people here are wishing she had been," said Eliza, looking pointedly at Casey now. Eliza pushed a silky strand of pale blonde hair over a shoulder then rolled her big blue eyes for drama. "Some people might be wishing that Taylor had never come back."

Casey just stared down at her bowl of untouched oatmeal. Her face looked even paler now, and DJ knew that she was thinking about the police and the possible charges that could be pressed.

"Taylor might forgive Casey," said Rhiannon in a hopeful tone.

Eliza laughed. "Are you talking about *our* Taylor? Taylor the witch-girl Mitchell?"

"You never know," said Rhiannon. "People can change."

Just then they heard Grandmother's voice speaking to Taylor. "It's so good to have all my girls back together again," she said as they entered the dining room like royalty. "Such beautiful girls," she continued as she gracefully pulled out her chair at the head of the table and slipped into it. "And I have a wonderful announcement to make." DJ hoped that it was the news that Taylor had indeed decided to let bygones be bygones and to forget that Casey was the one who had sabotaged her on MySpace. But then DJ realized that Taylor probably didn't even know that it was Casey who'd done it.

"On this fine morning when we welcome our long-lost Taylor back," began Grandmother, "I am also pleased to announce that you girls have been invited to participate in the Founder's Day Fashion Show."

DJ let out an involuntary groan, and Grandmother's brow, which had missed its regular Botox treatment, creased deeply.

"It is a high honor to be invited to participate in this event," continued Grandmother. "In the past it has been only the local debutantes who are included in this event. But, thankfully, my good friend Mrs. Vanderzan has taken notice of the lovely Carter House girls, and she would like to include you all in the fashion show lineup. And since this event coincides with homecoming weekend, it's a perfect fit to have you girls participate." Grandmother actually clapped her hands now. "So, as you girls can imagine, we have much to do in the next several weeks."

"What if we don't want to participate?" asked DJ.

Grandmother gave her an icy look. "Of course, you'll want to participate, Desiree. After all, the proceeds for this event go to a very good cause."

"What's that?" asked DJ.

Her grandmother looked slightly perplexed. "Well, I can't recall at the moment, but I happen to know that it is always a very worthwhile charity. I believe that last year's contributions were donated to the local animal shelter."

DJ grimaced at the thought that being tortured in a fashion show would somehow feed a stray cat. Not that she didn't care about stray animals—she certainly did; but she would rather scrub out stinky dog kennels than parade herself across some runway for a bunch of stuffy, rich town ladies. She hoped she could come up with a way to get out of this later—jump a freighter to China perhaps?

"Well now, Taylor," said Eliza in her sweet southern drawl. "Long time no see. How've you been doing anyway?"

"Fine." Taylor took a piece of dry toast and broke it in half.

"Where have you been?" asked Kriti with open curiosity. Her dark eyes studied Taylor closely, as if she were trying to figure out the mystery girl. Kriti and Taylor actually had similar coloring, since Kriti was Indian, but that is where their similarities ended.

Taylor tossed Kriti a warning frown. "None of your business."

Grandmother cleared her throat, but said nothing.

Taylor looked up at Eliza as if they had all been talking about nothing more than last Friday's high school football game. "I assume that Mr. Harper is still casting for *South Pacific* today?"

"He is," said Eliza coolly.

"We all think that Eliza will be cast as Nellie," added Rhiannon.

"And Rhiannon tried out for Liat," announced Eliza. Her eyes were locked on Taylor now. This was the role that Taylor had hoped to get. And to be fair, Taylor was a perfect typecast for the Polynesian beauty.

Taylor's arched brows lifted slightly higher. "Rhiannon as Liat? That seems a bit of a stretch."

"She has the voice for it," said DJ.

"I'd obviously need a wig and makeup." Rhiannon looked uncomfortable. "Besides, nothing has been decided," she said quickly.

"That's fortunate." Taylor nodded smugly.

"And, really," continued Rhiannon. "I mostly wanted to work on sets and costumes anyway."

"Good for you," said Taylor, again a bit too smugly. DJ wondered if Taylor really thought she had bagged that role, especially after being gone most of the week. Sure, the girl could sing and act and even looked the part, but to have that much confidence—well, it just made DJ's teeth hurt.

Then, suddenly it was time to head out for school, and the usual mad rush for purses and jackets and last-minute mirror checks kicked into full gear. Once they were outside, everyone except Taylor made a mad dash for Eliza's car.

Taylor casually got in DJ's car, acting like it was no big deal for everyone else to opt to ride with Eliza today. Never mind that they were packed like sardines into Eliza's small, white Porsche. Of course, DJ wasn't surprised that no one wanted to ride with Taylor and her. But as she started the car, she

20

wondered if perhaps this might be a nice opportunity for her to gently break the news about Casey's involvement in the MySpace incident. And not to get Casey in hot water, but DJ felt fairly certain that Taylor would hear it from someone at school anyway. In fact, it wouldn't surprise DJ if Taylor heard from the police before the day was over.

"So," DJ said as she backed out of the driveway. "I don't suppose you ever figured out who was behind the MySpace scam, did you?"

Taylor quickly turned to look at DJ. "Do you know?"

DJ kept her eyes on the road. "If it makes you feel any better, Taylor, she is really, really sorry."

"It wasn't you, was it?" asked Taylor in a voice that sounded slightly rattled and not like Taylor's normally assured self.

"No. Of course not."

"Oh."

"But it is someone we know."

"You mean someone from right here in town?" ventured Taylor. "Someone from Crescent Cove?"

"Yes."

"I thought it might've been someone from my old high school, you know, back in California."

DJ could tell that Taylor's guard was down, ever so slightly. Even so, DJ was determined to tread carefully. "No, it was actually someone from the house, Taylor. And just so you know, the only reason she did it was because of what happened with you and Bradford. She—"

"Rhiannon?" Taylor sounded shocked now.

"No. Not Rhiannon. She's not like that." DJ took in a quick breath. "It was Casey, Taylor, and it was simply because she felt sorry for—"

"Casey!" Taylor slapped her forehead. "Of course. That little lowlife loser. I should've known it was her."

"She's not a lowlife loser. And she's very sorry."

"Not as sorry as she's going to be." Taylor's voice was smooth and cold now, with a lethal edge to it.

DJ swallowed hard. What exactly did Taylor have in mind?

"I should've known it was her from the start," continued Taylor. "It's just her style to pull a chickenhearted stunt like that. Sneaky little lowlife loser girl!"

DJ was feeling desperate now. Why did Taylor have to act like this? "Casey wasn't thinking. She just felt sorry for Rhiannon. We all did."

"You weren't involved in the MySpace thing, were you?"

"No. I already told you that."

Taylor nodded. "Only Casey would sink that low."

"Only because she wanted to take revenge for Rhiannon." DJ slowed down for the intersection. "What you did to Rhiannon was wrong, Taylor."

"Not as wrong as what Casey did to me. That wasn't just wrong, it was illegal. And Casey is going to be one sorry—"

"You're not going to press charges, are you?"

"I most certainly am."

"But, Taylor, Casey is really—"

"I've heard enough about stupid Casey. If she were really sorry, she'd speak to me herself, DJ."

"She's probably afraid of you."

Taylor laughed. "She ought to be, that stupid little cowardly snake."

DJ knew it was useless. As soon as they were at school and parted ways, she called Casey on her cell phone. They weren't supposed to have them on at school, but classes hadn't started yet.

"Hey," said Casey in a dejected tone. "What's up, DJ?"

"Taylor," said DJ quickly. "I sort of broke the news to—"

"You told her it was me?"

"Well, she was going to find out. I thought maybe I could soften things."

"Did you?"

"Not exactly."

"How not exactly?"

"She is *really ticked*, Casey."

"I figured."

DJ didn't know what to say. She was afraid to tell Casey too much, worried that Casey might freak.

"She's going to press charges, isn't she?"

"It sounds like it."

"Well, that settles it then."

"Settles what?" DJ braced herself.

"I mean, at least I know where I stand. I've already confessed. All Taylor needs to do is press charges." Casey's voice broke. "I really am toast."

"You better call your parents, Casey."

"Yeah, I know."

"Maybe they can get you a lawyer."

Casey kind of laughed. "I guess I've finally proved it to them."

"Proved what?"

"That I really am the black sheep."

"Oh, you're not—"

"I better go," Casey said quickly. "Talk to you later."

DJ said good-bye, closed her phone, turned it off, and slid it into her bag. This was not going well.

"Hey, DJ," said Eliza as she joined her in the hallway. "Going my way?"

23

"Duh." They both had English Lit for first period.

"Who were you talking to?" asked Eliza. "It looked serious."

DJ told her about the Taylor/Casey scenario.

"Man, I would hate to be in Casey's shoes right now." Then Eliza kind of laughed. "Well, I mean, besides the fact that they are Doc Martens and remind me of army boots."

DJ shook her head. Why had she expected anything more from Eliza? That girl never seemed to take anything too seriously—well, unless it directly involved Eliza. But then Eliza had grown up in the lap of luxury. She'd been raised to be a princess. Why should her nonchalance about someone else's misfortune surprise DJ?

After DJ was seated in English Lit, she said a silent prayer for Casey, begging God to do something—and to do it fast—and to do it before Casey did something even more stupid.

3

HOMECOMING QUEEN

"HEY, GOOD LOOKING," said Conner as he came up behind DJ in the cafeteria. He slipped his arm around her shoulder, giving her a friendly little squeeze. "Where you been hiding out?"

DJ narrowed her eyes slightly. "I have *not* been hiding."

"But you *are* grumpy." He frowned then smiled in a teasing sort of way. "Probably because your old friend Taylor is back in town. I saw her in chemistry, and it looked like she must've enjoyed her vacation."

"If you think that's true, you should've seen her last night. And, for the record, yes, I am a little grumpy." She forced a smile. "Sorry about that. But it seems like this whole thing is about to explode, and it feels like I'm doing damage control."

"Don't worry so much." He leaned over and pecked her on the cheek. "I don't like seeing my favorite girl all stressed out."

"It's just that I feel like I'm caught in the middle."

"Well, didn't I try to convince you that Taylor was perfectly fine?" He jabbed her gently with an elbow. "And you were so certain she'd been abducted. So, where was she hiding anyway?"

"She's not saying." Then DJ told him about Taylor's threats against Casey.

"Poor Casey," he said with genuine concern. "But, really, she should've known better. The law is really starting to tighten down on Internet crimes."

"I know. But she thought she was doing it for Rhiannon."

"What a mess." He nodded now like he was beginning to understand her concerns.

DJ glanced around the cafeteria for Casey, but didn't see her anywhere. She was probably trying to keep a low profile for a while. DJ didn't blame her. Conner and DJ got their lunches and went over to sit at the table where Eliza and Harry were already seated. Kriti and Rhiannon soon joined them, and it seemed that all anyone wanted to talk about was Taylor and Casey. Everyone speculated over which way it was going to go, but everyone agreed that it was not looking good for Casey.

"We probably won't be seeing much of her," said DJ. "I think she plans to lie low."

"Speaking of going underground," said Eliza, "where is Taylor?"

"Probably pressing charges," said Kriti. "In geometry, she told me that Casey is going to get what's coming to her."

"I feel so sorry for Casey," said Rhiannon sadly. "I wish I could do something."

"I don't think anyone can help her now," said Conner.

"Besides a good lawyer," said Eliza.

"The girl is going down," said Harry.

"Hey, here comes Taylor now," said Conner.

"Hi, kiddies," said Taylor as she took an empty chair next to DJ. "What's up?"

"We're wondering the same thing," said DJ. "What's up with you?"

"Yeah," said Conner. "Did you call the cops on Casey yet?"

"As a matter of fact, I left a message with Detective Howard at the CCPD," said Taylor.

"What did you tell him?" asked DJ.

"Just that I'd suffered a little breakdown as a result of the Internet harassment and that was the reason I'd been missing. I'm sure he'll understand."

DJ swallowed hard. "Yeah, I'll bet."

"And I left another message with my mother's attorney."

"About what?" asked Eliza with catlike curiosity.

"What do you think?" Taylor opened her water bottle.

"So . . . you're really taking Casey down then?" asked Harry.

Taylor nodded firmly. "Oh, yeah."

"No room in that cold, cold heart of yours for forgiveness then?" ventured Conner.

She glared at him then peeled off the top of her yogurt container.

"What if Casey apologized?" asked DJ hopefully. She'd been thinking about what Taylor had said in the car this morning, about Casey being too cowardly to apologize.

Taylor's eyes glinted. "Oh, she already apologized."

DJ blinked. "She did?"

"Sure. Just a few minutes ago." Taylor held up her spoon as if to study it. "She came to me with tears and everything. She even promised to make a public statement to the whole school, confessing to everything."

"And you just blew her off?" said Conner.

"Pretty much." Taylor stuck a spoon in her yogurt and stirred.

"Wow," said Harry with his hands held up like he was feigning fear, "remind me not to step on your toes."

"That's right," said Taylor. "People who mess with me are just begging for trouble."

"Hey," said Eliza. "On a lighter note, I hear that nominations for homecoming queen start up next week." Then she sighed as if this was sad news. "You know what, ya'll? I've always dreamed of being homecoming queen. And now that I'm the new girl, I won't even have a ghost of a chance."

"Says who?" demanded Harry. "I'll nominate you."

"You will?" She beamed at him.

"It'll take more than that to make it as a finalist," said Conner. "The fight for homecoming queen can be fierce in this town."

"How do you know?" asked DJ.

"Trust me. I know," said Conner. "Remember, I have sisters."

"I think Eliza would make a great homecoming queen," said Kriti. "I'll vote for you, Eliza."

"Well, thank you very much." Eliza grinned. "And how about the rest of you? Would you vote for me too?"

Everyone sort of shrugged and halfheartedly agreed to vote for her, and thankfully the bell rang and lunchtime was over. DJ thought Eliza was crazy to want to run for homecoming queen. Why put yourself through that sort of pain on purpose?

"I just can't quit thinking about poor Casey," said Rhiannon as she and DJ trudged toward the drama department.

"I know."

"She won't do anything stupid, will she?"

"Huh?" DJ turned to look at Rhiannon.

"You know, like what Taylor did."

"You mean like run away?"

Rhiannon nodded. "I mean, she seemed so desperate when I saw her this morning, right after you told her what Taylor had said. She reminded me of a cornered animal. And she said that she couldn't stand being locked up somewhere, even if it was juvenile detention."

DJ shifted her purse strap to her other shoulder. "She probably won't get locked up."

"She will if Taylor gets her way. That girl is out for blood."

"I can't believe that Casey apologized like that and Taylor still wouldn't consider forgiving her."

"Better change the subject," warned Rhiannon. "Here comes Taylor now."

Taylor joined them as they entered the auditorium, acting as if nothing was wrong. She gabbed on about how excited she was about her audition for Liat today. "I can't imagine that Mr. Harper would consider anyone else." She smiled at Rhiannon as they took their seats. "I mean you probably would've made an okay Liat, but that was only because I was out of the picture. Now that's not the case. You don't mind, do you?"

As students continued to trickle in, Mr. Harper took center stage. "As you know, we have finished with our auditions and it's—"

"Excuse me, Mr. Harper," said Taylor from her front-and-center seat, raising her hand in the air. "I've been absent, but I really had hoped to audition for the role of Liat."

He peered into the audience. "Oh, Taylor. You're back."

"Is it too late?"

He paused as if considering. "No, of course not. Come on down and give it a try. You already impressed us with your general audition. Let's see how well you can do Liat."

So, slightly bowing to the audience like she was already a star, Taylor went down and, without any musical accompaniment or anything, flawlessly performed one of Liat's songs from the musical. Everyone clapped with enthusiasm, and Taylor smiled with such confidence that DJ knew she thought she had bagged this.

DJ was not so sure. Rhiannon had done a lovely rendition of Liat too. In fact, Rhiannon's sweet countenance and innocent personality made her far more like the Liat character than Taylor. Still, it wasn't DJ's decision.

"Thank you very much," said Mr. Harper after the applause stopped. "Now, I would like to make my announcements."

No one was very surprised when Eliza was cast in the lead as Nellie, the perky Navy nurse from Arkansas.

There were some murmurs of surprise when Sean Marscolli, a talented actor but a little on the short and pudgy side, was cast as Eliza's romantic interest and plantation owner, Emile. Eliza, however, took this news in a good-natured way, probably drawing from her solid southern roots of gentility and social graces.

Next, Bradford Wales was cast as Lieutenant Joe Cable, the romantic interest for Liat's character. DJ tried not to frown at this. But all she could think was how unfair it would be if Taylor got the part of Liat and now Bradford, the boy Taylor had stolen from Rhiannon, would be her love interest.

Mr. Harper read off a few more roles, and DJ was relieved that she was only going to be in a very minor role—Ensign Cora McRae, whoever that was supposed to be.

Finally Mr. Harper cleared his throat as if he were about to make an important announcement. "As some of you perhaps have guessed, I've been giving myself a little extra time to consider the role of our sweet, young Liat. I have decided to stick with my first instincts in casting for this role. I have decided that Rhiannon Farley will play Liat, and for—"

DJ couldn't help herself. She actually started to clap, and loudly too. And so did several others. Enough so that Mr. Harper quit speaking. But when DJ glanced over at Taylor, she

30

saw that her roommate was scowling darkly. Clearly, Taylor was not the least bit pleased by this surprising announcement.

"Yes," continued Mr. Harper, smiling on stage as if he had just made a great performance himself. "I can see that some of you agree with me on this choice. And, while I must admit that Miss Mitchell did give me some pause, for she did a wonderful audition, I would prefer to cast Taylor in a much larger role, a very important role. I have cast Taylor Mitchell as Bloody Mary." He beamed at Taylor like she should be thrilled with this news.

"Bloody Mary?" said Taylor with disgust. "Liat's mother? She's a fat cow. No way am I playing her."

Mr. Harper chuckled. "Well, it's certainly not a typecast, Taylor. But Bloody Mary sings some wonderful songs, and with your voice — "

"Forget it," snapped Taylor, tightly folding her arms across her chest. "I would rather paint scenery than play Bloody Mary."

This news had to be making Camilla Fairbanks happy. She had tried out for Bloody Mary, and everyone had assumed she was a shoe in. Her singing voice wasn't anything like Taylor's, but Camilla had the physique and the loudness to go with the role.

"Well, no one can force you to play a part you don't want," said Mr. Harper a bit stiffly. "Although, I should warn you, attitude will reflect on your final grade, Miss Mitchell. And that goes for everyone. We are a team, and we're all in this production together. We don't have room for prima donnas."

Taylor just tilted her nose in the air.

DJ, though, couldn't help but grin. This was just too funny, and it was all she could do not to burst out laughing. Poetic justice, at last! For a refreshing change it seemed that Taylor was not coming out on top after all. Taylor had finally gotten what she deserved.

Of course, DJ felt bad as she reminded herself that Taylor hadn't always come out on top. In fact, Taylor had confessed some hard things to DJ, back before the Internet scandal and before she'd run away and been missing. Still, the way Taylor had been treating Casey today—well, DJ couldn't help but be a little bit glad.

The class was separated into various rehearsal groups. Since DJ's role included, of all things, dancing, she was sent off with the dancers to learn some steps. Ironically, it was kind of fun; maybe because, much to her own surprise, DJ wasn't half bad at it. When class finally ended, she was warm, and her cheeks were flushed.

"Did you hear the news?" said Eliza as she came back to where DJ was getting a long, cold drink at the water fountain.

"About what?" DJ stood up and looked curiously at Eliza.

"About Liat."

DJ frowned and wondered if Eliza was feeling okay. "Yes, Eliza," she said slowly. "We all heard about that. Remember? Rhiannon got cast as Liat, and Taylor threw a hissy fit."

"Not *that*," whispered Eliza. "I mean, did you hear that Rhiannon made a deal with Taylor."

"A deal?"

Eliza lowered her voice as if she thought someone else was listening. "Rhiannon offered Taylor the role of Liat if Taylor would promise not to press charges against Casey."

"No way!"

Eliza nodded with large blue eyes. "Way."

"And Taylor agreed?"

"She did. I heard the whole thing myself."

DJ didn't know whether to be happy or ticked. On one hand, this might get Casey off the hook—that is if Taylor stuck to her word. On the other hand, Taylor, once again, came out on top. Not only did she get the role she wanted, she also got Rhiannon's ex-boyfriend, the guy Taylor had already stolen once, for her love interest. If DJ's memory served, they even had a fairly passionate kissing scene. "Man," said DJ with a frown. "Sometimes life sucks."

"Not according to Taylor," said Eliza. "She's already worked it out with Mr. Harper, and she's flying high."

"I can just imagine."

"And I have a feeling Taylor will stick to her agreement too. I mean, that girl may be a lot of things, but I think she's fairly honest."

"Hey," DJ said, "I gotta call Casey and tell her the good news." DJ dialed Casey's cell phone number, but not surprisingly, Casey's phone was off. "I gotta go." She took off jogging toward the locker bay. And, sure enough, there was Casey with her head in her locker, trying to shove a notebook onto an already jammed shelf.

"Casey," said DJ breathlessly. "Have you heard?"

Casey pushed in the notebook and slammed the locker shut. "What?" she asked in a flat-toned voice.

"It's over. Taylor is playing Liat in exchange for everything. Rhiannon made a deal with her—for you!"

Casey looked confused. "Rhiannon did what?"

"She gave up her role in *South Pacific*! She handed over the part Taylor wanted in exchange for Taylor's promise not to press charges against you."

"Seriously? And Taylor agreed?"

"Yes. She really wanted that role. Plus, Bradford is playing Joe Cable, Taylor's character's love interest."

Casey frowned and shook her head. "That's kind of like twisting the knife for Rhiannon, isn't it?"

"I know."

"It figures that Taylor would use this for her own gain."

"Still, it's good news. This thing with you and Taylor is over now."

Casey nodded slowly, as if taking this in, but she still didn't look fully convinced. "Maybe round one is over, but I doubt that it's completely over."

"You're probably right, but at least the legal part of it might be over. Eliza and I both think Taylor will keep her word."

Casey brightened slightly. "And that is a relief. I mean, I so did not want to be locked up. The idea of being stuck in some kind of detention facility was freaky. But, man, do I owe Rhiannon now."

"That's for sure," said DJ. "That was a huge sacrifice on her part."

Casey sighed. "I wonder why life has to be so complicated."

"Especially when you don't allow God be part of it," pointed out DJ. She and Rhiannon had been working on Casey . . . trying her to get her life right with God. Maybe this would be the real turning point.

"So, are you going to start preaching at me now?"

"Not right now," said DJ, grinning. "I have to get to class." But as DJ hurried off she knew Casey was going to have to listen to someone's "preaching." And considering Rhiannon's sacrifice, Casey ought to be willing to listen to her.

"I can't believe you're sticking with volleyball," Taylor said in a tone that suggested disgust. She was getting dressed following PE, their last class. And, although DJ had been trying to avoid Taylor since drama, she now felt cornered as she laced up her volleyball shoes.

"I like it," DJ said with her head down, focusing on her laces.

"Why?" demanded Taylor.

DJ wanted to ask Taylor why she needed to know but suspected it was simply Taylor's smokescreen, a way to avoid other topics that might not be so comfortable — like where were you these past few days or how did it feel to be cast as Bloody Mary until Rhiannon struck a deal? "It's fun," DJ said.

"Getting sweaty and hanging with jock girls is fun?" Taylor buttoned her shirt.

"And it's a good form of exercise." DJ was losing patience. And so she tossed a slightly accusatory look at Taylor. "Anyway, it beats having to constantly diet or play with anorexia like *some* girls I won't mention."

Taylor scowled. "I don't *play with anorexia*, DJ."

DJ shrugged. "Maybe not, but you always act like you have some big phobia when it comes to eating good food."

Taylor smoothed her fitted shirt over her long, lean waist. "I avoid fats and carbs because I happen to *care* about my appearance."

"And I happen to care about my *health*," said DJ. "I'd rather eat normal foods and participate in sports than constantly be on a diet."

Taylor gave DJ her haughty look now. "Well, if you don't mind having a lesbian coach gaping at you, I guess sports are okay."

DJ sucked in a quick breath, glancing over her shoulder just in case Coach Jones was around to hear that mean comment. "You don't know if that's true, Taylor."

Taylor shrugged. "I don't know that it's not."

"You must've forgotten how it feels to have people believing mean lies about you."

Taylor's brow creased slightly. She actually seemed to be considering this.

DJ drove home her point. "It seems like you'd have more compassion."

"I think I liked you better before you became such a goody-two-shoes, DJ." Then Taylor picked up her black Kate Spade bag, slung it over her shoulder, and walked off, her high heels clicking across the hard locker-room floor.

A few minutes later, Casey came into the locker room, glancing nervously around. "I wanted to make sure that Taylor was gone before I came in," she said to DJ.

"Coast is clear," said DJ. "Thank goodness she left when she did. I felt like I wanted to deck her."

Casey's eyebrows shot up. "Really? Why?"

DJ quietly filled her in on Taylor's derogatory comment about Coach Jones.

"Well, a lot of people think that's true," said Casey. "In fact, I've even heard you make some of those same kinds of comments."

"Only as a joke!" DJ's face went red. "Well, I'm not going to do it anymore."

Casey just shrugged. "Whatever."

"Think about it, Casey. No one likes to be judged, not to mention *misjudged*."

Casey pulled on her shorts. "I guess. Even so, I keep my distance from Coach."

DJ rolled her eyes.

"I'm just saying."

DJ let it go. Still, she was determined to watch her words a little more closely. And even as they did their regular drills, ending with a match between JV and Varsity, DJ sensed that her attitude toward her teammates, even the "jock girls" as Taylor liked to call them, was changing. She was accepting them, and they were accepting her—like a real team—and that felt good.

"Great game, Tawnee," said DJ after Varsity won, and they were all heading back to the locker room. "Way to be on it."

Tawnee looked surprised, but then smiled. "Thanks!"

Since DJ hadn't seen Conner since lunch, she had asked Casey to join her in watching the end of his soccer practice. But as the girls emerged from the locker room, there was Conner waiting for her in the gym's breezeway. "Hey, girls," he said cheerfully as he pushed back his damp hair. "How was practice?"

"Okay," said DJ. Conner slipped an arm around DJ's waist and gave her a squeeze. DJ smiled. Having a boyfriend was nice, but it still took some getting used to.

"Better than okay," said Casey, "since we quit early."

"Same with us. Coach cut practice short because we have two back-to-back matches tomorrow morning."

Just then Garrison McKinley joined them. He looked fresh out of the shower room too. "Hey, ladies," he said, smiling at Casey. "What's up?"

DJ and Casey chatted with the guys as the four of them walked out to the parking lot. Then Garrison brushed his fingers through Casey's short hair and chuckled. "Gotta admire a girl who isn't afraid to look butch."

"What?" Casey turned and glared at him.

But Garrison just smiled "Hey, if you're pretty enough, you can carry it off."

"Meaning what?" demanded Casey.

"Meaning you can carry it off."

Casey looked unconvinced, but DJ was certain that Garrison was totally flirting with Casey.

"Go easy on Casey," warned DJ. "She's had a rough day."

"Could've been rougher," added Conner.

Now they were all standing around DJ's car, and the guys were still making small talk like they weren't ready to say good-bye yet. And it seemed that Casey was actually warming up to Garrison now, like maybe the light had clicked on and she'd figured out that he was pretty interested in her.

Garrison mentioned a movie that had just released. "Hey, you guys want to go together?" he asked. "I mean, the four of us?"

DJ peered curiously at Casey. Garrison was obviously asking her out but trying to keep it casual. And, unfortunately for Garrison, Casey started to act oblivious again, giving him a blank expression. Or maybe she just wanted to be asked out properly.

"Sounds good to me," said DJ. "I know I've been wanting to see that film."

"Me too," added Conner.

"So how about you, Casey?" asked Garrison hopefully.

But now Casey was staring in the other direction, away from the group and toward the street, and DJ was getting seriously irritated. Why was Casey being so stubborn about this? DJ turned and followed Casey's gaze in time to see a small child about to step into the street where traffic, oblivious to school-zone laws, was rapidly approaching.

Without thinking or even saying a word—DJ took off. Sprinting as fast as she could, she raced toward the child, who was nearly in the middle of the street now.

"Look out!" she screamed as she leaped. With arms outstretched like she was diving for a low shot, she grabbed the little boy and pushed him straight toward the curb. In that same instant, a blur of shining metal charged directly into her. And suddenly everything went from light to fuzzy to black.

"Is she okay?" said a woman's voice. "It happened so quickly. I didn't even see her."

DJ opened her eyes to see a dark-haired woman putting a blanket over her. Then she noticed Conner was there too, holding her hand in his.

"What happened?" she muttered.

"You were hit by a car, DJ." His eyes were serious. "Don't move. Garrison already called 911, and an ambulance is coming."

Then DJ tried to sit up, but a jolt of sharp pain surged through her left leg and she immediately leaned back again, dizzy with pain.

"Just be still," said Conner.

"Seriously, DJ," said Casey from the other side. She gently moved some hair from DJ's eyes. "Don't move, okay?"

DJ closed her eyes and mumbled okay. Or at least she thought she did, and once again things got blurry.

5

THE TRIP TO THE HOSPITAL was hazy, but DJ vaguely remembered the ambulance's siren, sort of like an alarm clock that's been shoved beneath the pillow but still buzzing.

At the hospital, she did her best to cooperate with doctors and nurses and X-ray technicians and others as they examined and moved her from room to room in what seemed some sort of strange chess game or medical maze. It felt slightly surreal, or maybe that was from the pain medication they gave her. At times she almost felt as if she were watching this happening to someone else—or maybe she'd fallen asleep watching *Gray's Anatomy* again.

Then finally, with something stiff wrapped around the lower part of her leg and pillows propped beneath it, she was settled into yet another room. She fell asleep, and this time when she opened her eyes her grandmother was standing over her.

"Desiree," she said softly with a slight frown. "How are you feeling?"

"I've had better days." DJ looked around at the sparse, beige room with medical equipment all around. A nurse was standing nearby doing something on a laptop.

Grandmother nodded. "It seems you have suffered a broken leg, some cracked ribs, as well as a minor concussion."

DJ grimaced. "Is that all?"

"Are you in much pain?" Grandmother asked.

DJ started to nod then stopped. Her head hurt too much. "Yes," she muttered.

The nurse stepped over and held out two little white pills. "I've got something for that," she said. "But it might make you sleepy."

DJ didn't care. She thankfully took the pills with a sip of water and then closed her eyes again.

"Your friends are still here," said Grandmother. "They want to know if it's okay to see you."

DJ shrugged and then grimaced again. "It's okay with me," she said.

Casey, Conner, and Garrison came in and visited with her. But she was getting sleepy, and for the most part they chatted amongst themselves, making jokes about how they had missed the movie in order to play doctor. But it got harder to focus, and DJ felt herself drifting away. She was sorry to miss out on her friends, but it was nice to take a break from the pain.

When DJ awoke, the room was dark, and no one was in sight. She felt thirsty. A cup and a pitcher sat on the bedside table, and she fumbled to pour some water. Just as she took a sip, Casey emerged from the bathroom.

"You're awake," Casey said.

"Yeah," DJ said. "What time is it?"

"It's after nine."

"When do I go home?"

"Not tonight," said Casey. "I asked your grandmother if I could stay here with you, and she seemed relieved to go home. I get the impression that she doesn't like hospitals much."

"She hates hospitals. My mom told me that when Grandmother gets her plastic surgery done she goes to this special clinic that looks like a spa, and even then she has to take tranquilizers just to keep from freaking."

"I think I'd give up the plastic surgery if I were her," said Casey.

"Yeah, me too."

"So, how are you feeling?"

"Sore."

"I should warn you, the press came while you were asleep."

"The press?"

"You're a hero, DJ."

"Huh?"

"Remember, you saved that little boy."

"Oh, yeah. The little boy!" DJ couldn't believe she'd forgotten about that. "He's okay?"

"He's fine. It was Coach Jones's kid."

"Coach Jones has a kid?"

"Apparently."

"I didn't even know she was married."

"She's not." Casey grinned. "But if you haven't heard the news, you *can* have babies without being married."

DJ smiled.

"Anyway, she's been here too. Those big yellow flowers are from her."

DJ looked over to where several bouquets were lined up by the window. "Oh."

"Yeah. You've had quite a few visitors. But we've kept them at bay."

"Did Conner go home?"

"He didn't want to, but I said he should. He's got those soccer matches tomorrow." Casey brightened now. "Hey, Garrison *likes* me."

"I know."

"How do you know?"

"It's one of the things I remember before I jumped in front of that truck."

"It was an SUV."

"SUV, truck, whatever. It felt like a locomotive."

"Did your grandmother tell you that you're scheduled for surgery at six in the morning?"

"Huh?"

"Yeah. They're going to put a piece of metal in your leg. Apparently that's the latest thing for getting broken bones to heal up more quickly."

For the first time that day, DJ felt tears filling her eyes. "I can't believe this all happened to me, Casey. I mean, one minute I'm just living a normal life, and the next minute I'm—I'm—" And now she was crying.

Casey handed her the tissue box. "It's going to be okay, DJ. Seriously, you could've been killed. I heard the doctor saying it was good that you're in such great shape and that most people would've been a lot more messed up than you are. He told your grandmother that you were lucky you only broke your fibula and not your tibia."

"What's that mean?"

"It means you broke the smaller bone in your leg. And apparently it was a clean break, whatever that means. Anyway, he said the prognosis was very good."

"But look at me." DJ blotted her tears. "I'm an invalid."

"Hey, you're lucky you're not a vegetable."

DJ blew her nose.

"Seriously, DJ, we saw the whole thing, and we thought you were about to be history. By the time we reached you, which seemed to take forever—like who knew you could run that fast—I honestly thought you were dead. I don't think I've ever been so scared in my life." Casey shook her head.

"I guess I should be glad to be alive ..." DJ forced a weak smile for her friend's benefit.

"Just so you know," Casey continued, "the other girls at the house send their love. Every one of them has either called or stopped by." She made a face. "Even Taylor acted all concerned when she came. She insisted that she had to see you, but I had already told Eliza to tell everyone it would be better to wait until tomorrow. That's what the nurse told me to tell them. And so I had to turn her away. I hope you don't mind."

"I think I've been too out of it to mind." DJ sighed. "But thanks for sticking around, Casey."

"There's no way I was leaving you here alone."

"I appreciate it." DJ thought about her mom, wondering if she would've been here right now if DJ had died after getting hit by that car. Too bad she hadn't had one of those near-death experiences where you briefly visit loved ones in heaven. That would've been pretty cool. She wondered what Mom would've said to her. She probably would've welcomed her, hugged her, and stroked her hair like she used to do when DJ was little. Then maybe she would've sent her back. Thinking of Mom reminded DJ of her dad. What would he think about this? Would he care? Did he even know?

"Uh, Casey," DJ began hesitantly. "Do you think Grand-mother told my dad about the accident?"

"I don't know, but it seems like she would've. Do you want me to call and ask her?" Casey started to dig in her backpack.

"No." DJ held a hand up to stop her. "That's okay."

"Want me to call him for you?" Casey pulled out her cell phone and opened it.

DJ shook her head. "To be honest, I don't think I really care whether he knows or not. It's not like he can do anything." Or like he would do anything ... besides having his wife send flowers or a card."

"Okay, if you're sure." She closed the phone.

DJ didn't like to think about her dad. And she certainly didn't want to talk to him. What if he did something out of character and decided to fly out here? How weird would that be? Seriously, the last thing she needed right now was for him to show up and act like "the loving father."

DJ was glad Casey was staying the night. Somehow she didn't like the idea of being at the hospital alone. DJ had never been in a hospital overnight. "Where are you sleeping tonight?"

Casey pointed to the vacant bed on the other side of the room. "The nurse said I can sleep there if I want to."

"Roommates again." DJ forced a smile.

"That's right." Casey smiled. "Oh, and the nurse said you're not supposed to eat anything tonight. For your surgery in the morning, you know. And no fluids after midnight. Just the IV. Hope that's okay."

"I'm not hungry." DJ closed her eyes. As much as she wanted to be brave, and as much as she wanted to be thankful that she wasn't severely injured or even dead, she mostly felt sorry for herself. Why had this happened to her? Why hadn't God been watching out for her better? And how long would she be laid up with a broken leg and cracked ribs? Obviously, she would miss the rest of volleyball season. Maybe even spring soccer too. Why was life so unfair?

DJ barely opened her eyes when the nurse woke her up the next morning. It took about an hour to get her prepped for surgery, and by the time they wheeled her into the operating room, everything was getting fuzzy again. Then a guy came over and talked to her about breathing and asked her to count backward from ten. She barely reached six when everything slipped away. The next thing she knew she was in what she was informed was a recovery room.

"What about the surgery?" she asked groggily.

The nurse smiled. "It's all done, dear. It went well."

After a couple more naps, a vaguely familiar white-haired surgeon came to talk to her. "You're fortunate that it was a clean break," he said. "And with the rod now in place, you should be up and moving around in no time."

"Really?" DJ blinked. "Will I be able to play volleyball this season?"

"Well, not this season, but next year."

"Oh."

"You'll be on crutches for a few weeks, along with a walking boot. You'll also need some physical therapy, which we'll start up first thing next week."

"Crutches might be cool." DJ could imagine herself zinging through the hallways at school.

"And the scarring should be minimal," the doctor said.

"Scarring?"

"From the surgery. Your grandmother was concerned about the appearance of your legs, Desiree." He winked at her in a grandfatherly sort of way.

DJ gave him a smirk. "My grandmother is *all* about appearances."

"Naturally, there is a lot of bruising simply from being hit by the car, and also some swelling from the surgery. But the scar from the incision shouldn't be too noticeable after a month or so. Especially since I glued it closed."

DJ blinked. "You *glued* it?"

He chuckled. "Yes. It's a new technique. No stitches or staples. It's a kind of superglue that completely closes the wound. It's a great way to ward off infection, plus you can shower without covering it."

"So you put me back together with a rod and superglue?"

"Something like that."

"How long will I be in the hospital?"

"If all goes well, we might get you released later this afternoon." He made some final notes on her file then nodded. "As long as you promise to take it easy when you get home. That means no foot races or shenanigans."

She assured him that would not be a problem and then, as she was being wheeled back to her room, she noticed a party or something down the hall. But as she got closer she noticed that the crowd consisted of her friends from Carter House, as well as Conner and Harry and a couple of other guys. There were balloons and flowers and get-well signs, but perhaps most surprising was what appeared to be a camera crew milling about the hallway near her door—along with local celebrity Bonnie Hudson, anchor woman of the six o'clock news.

"Make way, everyone," ordered Eliza. She waved her arms as if directing traffic or perhaps she was simply trying to hog the cameras. "Let's give DJ some space," she commanded as DJ was wheeled into her room. Then Eliza actually shooed everyone out of the room. "Give us a few minutes, *please!*"

"What's going on?" DJ asked Eliza. The nurse and orderly were helping DJ settle into her bed, removing the IV tube, and getting her leg situated on some pillows.

"You mean besides a circus?" said the nurse as she finished up what she was doing. That's when Eliza came over and set her Gucci bag on the bedside table as if she were part of the medical staff too.

"What are you doing?" DJ asked Eliza. "Are you running the hospital now too?"

"No, I'm here to help you."

DJ shrugged then made a feeble wave to Casey, who was now seated in a chair by the window and wearing a slightly unhappy expression, as if she personally resented Eliza's little takeover. But at least she waved back.

"Bonnie Hudson is here to see you, DJ," Eliza informed her.

"So?" DJ stared at Eliza. "What's that got to do with you?"

"Well, we don't want you being filmed until we've fixed you up a little." Eliza removed a sleek-looking cosmetic bag from her purse then peered down at DJ with a concerned frown.

"It's okay." DJ felt silly over Eliza's focus on her appearance. "Really, I don't care how I look."

"No, dear, it's not okay." Now Eliza held up a hand mirror. "You should care how you look because, trust me, it's not even close to okay."

DJ was shocked to see her reflection. She did look pretty bad. Besides the flattened bed-head hair in need of a good shampoo, she had a brownish yellow bruise on the left side of her forehead and an ugly red abrasion across her cheek. Her lips were cracked and dry and there were even some white tracks of what must've been drool alongside both sides of her mouth. Not a pretty picture.

"See what I mean?" said Eliza.

"Uh-huh." And before DJ could say anything else, Eliza was carefully washing her face with a warm washcloth and then gently wiping on something that smelled like roses.

"You just sit still, dahling," Eliza said softly. "I'll have you as good as new in no time. Or almost."

After Eliza finished with her face, she fussed a bit with DJ's hair and finally handed the mirror back to DJ. "Better?"

DJ nodded. "Yeah. Thanks."

"Ready for your adoring fans?"

"I, uh, I guess."

"Okay. I'll tell them to take it easy on you." Then Eliza went and opened the door and, acting like DJ's personal publicity agent, she allowed the camera crew and reporter as well as Coach Jones and a slightly familiar looking little boy inside the room.

"I'm Bonnie Hudson," said the petite brunette that DJ already recognized from TV. "And I've been dying to talk to you, Desiree."

"DJ, please."

Bonnie smiled. "Sure, DJ. Well, DJ, *you* are the talk of the town today." She nodded to her crew, and DJ could tell that their cameras were already rolling. "Your grandmother, Mrs. Carter, gave us permission to speak to you, but I want to be sure you're okay with it too."

DJ shrugged. "I'm fine."

"Super." Bonnie waved over Coach Jones and a small boy with dark curls framing his pixie face. "Come on over here, Ms. Jones. I think it's high time for introductions."

Coach Jones looked slightly uncomfortable, but she forced a nervous smile. "Greetings, DJ. This is my little boy Jackson. He'll be four in January. And he has recently become your biggest fan."

"Hi, DJ," said the brown-faced little boy in a shy voice.

"Hey, Jackson," said DJ. "It's nice to meet you." She patted her bed. "Do you want to sit up here so I can see you better?"

"Okay." He waited for his mom to help him up then sat quietly looking at her with a somber expression.

"You're doing all right then?" asked DJ.

"Uh-huh." He nodded.

"You didn't get hurt?"

"Just here." He pointed to his elbow where a Big Bird bandage with was securely adhered.

"Ouch," DJ said.

"You saved my life." He looked at her with serious eyes.

"Oh, I don't know about that —"

"You did too," he said, a bit louder. "My mama says you're an angel."

DJ couldn't help but grin at Coach Jones now. "She did, did she?"

"That's what I heard, DJ," said Coach in a matter-of-fact tone. "Casey told me that you ran like the dickens and then did a dive that looked like you were flying."

DJ tried to shrug, but remembered how much it hurt to do that. "I only did what you taught me to do in volleyball."

Coach Jones turned to Bonnie now. "DJ is the star player of my varsity women's volleyball team. She will be sorely missed this season."

"I'll bet you're thankful just the same," said Bonnie.

Coach nodded with tears actually glistening in her eyes as she looked at DJ. "Oh, yes. I'm so very thankful. I just feel so badly that DJ has suffered as a result."

"Guess that proves I'm not a real angel," said DJ, smiling a little.

"Oh, yes you are," said Jackson stubbornly.

Bonnie asked just a few more questions, and finally the cameras were shut down. Bonnie shook DJ's hand. "It's a pleasure to meet a real hero, DJ. I hope you make a speedy recovery." Then the media exited, and DJ was left with Coach Jones and Jackson.

"I had no idea he was your son," said DJ. "Not that it made any difference. But I'm sure glad I saw him when I did. It all happened so quickly. I didn't have time to think or anything."

"Thank you again, DJ," said Coach. "I'm so glad you were there. My boyfriend had picked Jackson up from daycare for me. He was still in the parking lot, getting something out of his trunk, when Jackson took off across the street. I guess he figured I was over there in the gym."

DJ shook her finger at Jackson. "You really should know better than to run across the street like that."

"I'm sorry, DJ."

She softened now. "And you won't do it again, now will you?"

He solemnly shook his head. "No."

"I've told him before that he's never to cross the street without a grown-up," Coach said. "And he never had before."

"Well, I'm just glad you're okay," said DJ, running her fingers through his soft curly hair.

"Most people at school didn't even know I had a son," the coach said quietly. "But now they will."

"And they should," said DJ. "Jackson is a delightful guy. You should bring him to our games. Well, I guess *your* games, not *mine* anymore."

Coach Jones frowned. "That's such a shame, DJ. We really did need you this season. I hope you'll still come out and support the team anyway."

"Sure," said DJ. But she wasn't so sure. It would be hard being stuck on the sidelines.

"Well, I know your friends are eager to see you. There's quite a mob gathered out there."

"It's been a pleasure to meet you, Jackson," said DJ.

Then, to her surprise, he leaned over and gently kissed her on the cheek.

"Why, thank you," she told him.

"Thank you!" Coach said as she hefted up her son, smiling down on DJ. "We can never thank you enough, can we, Jackson?"

"Thank you, DJ," he called out sweetly as he waved his stubby fingers over his mom's shoulder.

"And don't let your adoring fans wear you out," warned Coach as she opened the door to allow the group inside.

6

homecoming queen

"WE NEED TO LIMIT THE VISITORS to three at a time," the nurse informed them as a group of about ten crowded around DJ's bed. DJ feigned disappointment, but she was actually relieved. All this attention was pretty overwhelming.

"I'll leave," offered Casey. "Since I got to spend the night with her."

"I'll go with Casey," said Garrison. Naturally this got some attention since it was still news that these two were becoming a couple. Finally the visitors dwindled down to just Conner and Eliza and Harry.

"We can pretend that this is a double date," joked Eliza as she pulled up a chair.

"Maybe I should order out some lunch for us," said Harry.

"I do feel hungry," admitted DJ. "What time is it anyway?"

"It's past eleven," said Eliza. "And I think I saw a food cart out there. Want me to go check?"

"Hospital food?" Conner made a face.

DJ wasn't so sure she cared.

"Hey, I could make a Hammerhead run," said Conner.

"Oh, man," said DJ. "Fish and chips?"

He nodded. "I could sneak it in here."

"You really want to eat all that fatty fried food?" asked Eliza.

DJ frowned. Both guys gave Eliza a warning look and, thankfully, she didn't push it.

"I'll call it in first," said Conner, reaching for his cell phone. Eliza and Harry joked with DJ as Conner made the call. Then they all talked for a while before Conner took off to get the order and others came back in to visit again.

"You need to clear out of here so she can eat her lunch in peace," the nurse warned Rhiannon, Casey, and Kriti after just a few minutes. DJ peeked at the food under the metal tray and pretended to be interested, but mostly she was thinking about fish and chips.

"Guess we'll see you back at the house," said Rhiannon. She put her hand on DJ's. "I'm so glad you're okay."

DJ thanked them and almost asked why Taylor hadn't come in to say hello, but didn't. She figured Taylor probably had "more important" things to do. But shortly after they left, Taylor slipped in by herself.

"I know you're supposed to be eating lunch—" she said quietly closing the door behind her.

"Nah, I'm not really eating that," DJ said. "Conner is getting me something at The Hammerhead Café."

"Good. I wanted to come say hi, but I figured it would be better if I came in alone since I'm pretty much being treated like a piranha by our so-called friends."

Taylor sat in the chair across her, crossing one leg over the other and carefully studying DJ. "You don't look too bad," she said.

"Thanks."

"You're sure getting a lot of attention."

"I guess." DJ almost reminded Taylor that she had been the one getting most of the attention last week, what with the MySpace thing and going missing. But suddenly that seemed like a long time ago. Funny how things can change so quickly.

"I actually felt pretty bad when I heard about it," said Taylor.

"Not as bad as I felt." DJ made a face.

"No, probably not. I can't imagine being hit by car." Taylor shook her head. "I don't really like pain."

"Who does?"

Taylor shrugged. "I guess there are a lot of kinds of pain."

DJ studied her for a long moment. "So, now that I'm laid up in a hospital bed—broken leg, cracked ribs—maybe I should play the sympathy card and ask you one more time: Where were you when you were gone last week?"

Taylor sighed. "It's not like it's a big deal, DJ. But if you must know … I can trust you not to go blabbing it around, right?"

"You can trust me."

"Yeah, I think I can." Still, Taylor didn't go on.

"So, where were you? I kept imagining you at some swanky five-star beach resort, with people waiting on you and stuff. Was it like that?"

Taylor laughed. "I was cooped up in a nasty motel room with cockroaches and smelly linens and a lot of alcohol."

"Seriously?"

Taylor nodded. "Yep. I pretty much drank and smoked and felt like giving up."

DJ frowned. "Giving up? What do you mean?"

Taylor waved her hand dismissively. "I mean temporary insanity. No big deal. Here I am, just fine and dandy, right?"

"I guess." But DJ was still curious. What did Taylor mean by giving up? "So, you must've been depressed." DJ peered at her.

57

"I can relate. I mean, last night when I realized what had really happened, the broken leg and everything—well, it was pretty depressing."

"Meaning you're not depressed about it now?" Taylor looked skeptical.

"Okay, I'm not exactly happy. But then, look at the bright side, I could've been killed. Or as Casey suggested, I could've been a vegetable."

"I'd rather be dead than a vegetable."

"Me too." DJ realized this was the most serious conversation she'd had with any of her friends today. The rest of them had been joking and lighthearted. "You know," she began slowly. "I felt kind of robbed that I didn't have one of those near-death experiences. You know what I mean?"

Taylor nodded. "I've read about that—people who are clinically dead for a few minutes and think they've seen heaven."

"Yeah, that would've been cool."

"You mean if it were real."

"People who experience it seem to think it's real."

"I know. I had a grandmother who believed in stuff like that."

"Had? As in she's not around anymore?"

"She died several years ago."

"Oh. Sorry." DJ tried to imagine Taylor with a grandmother. "Was she anything like my grandmother?"

"No one is quite like your grandmother."

DJ nodded. "That's true."

"Remember when I quoted the Bible to you?"

DJ nodded. Actually, that had been a real shocker. Who would've guessed that a girl like Taylor would even know what a Bible was? "Was that something you picked up from your grandmother?"

"She was a real church-going lady. And she tried to get me to follow in her footsteps."

"But you had other plans?"

"Not at first. But later on, after she was gone, I had to question a lot of that Christian nonsense. And finally I decided that's all it was—just nonsense."

"Lunch has arrived," announced Conner as he entered the room. Then he saw Taylor and frowned.

"And I'm just leaving," said Taylor. She stood and looped the strap of her bag over her shoulder, giving her long curls a toss. "Not that you two will miss me. See you later, DJ." Then she went out and closed the door with a suggestive little wink—like Conner and DJ actually planned to do something right there in the hospital room. Yeah, right!

"Good riddance," said Conner as he removed DJ's lunch tray and set the paper bags in its place.

"She's not so bad," said DJ.

"Compared to what?"

DJ shrugged. "Getting hit by a car?"

He laughed. "By the way, Eliza and Harry got sidetracked. I didn't think you'd mind if they didn't make it back."

DJ smiled in relief. "Not at all."

Then Conner laid out the fish and chips, which were still hot. Soon they were both happily eating. Still, DJ couldn't help but replay in her mind some of the things Taylor had said, or almost said.

It made her wonder.

By the time DJ got home, after cooperating with two more news interviews for other TV stations, followed by a very uncomfortable ride in the back of her grandmother's Mercedes, she felt more tired and sore than she had since the accident.

Casey had acted as nurse during the drive home, and then as her bodyguard as they slowly made their way into the house. DJ had to sit down on the front steps, easing herself up backward one slow step at a time, before Casey finally helped her stand and make her way through the door.

Grandmother led the girls into the main floor bedroom that previously had been inhabited by Inez, the housekeeper. "You will have to stay here for now, Desiree." Grandmother watched as Casey helped DJ settle into the twin-sized bed. "Inez will bunk with Clara—which should make everyone fairly miserable."

DJ was glad to see that the bedding was fresh; at least Inez wasn't bearing a grudge yet. Grandmother made an attempt to fluff a pillow. "And when you're able to manage the stairs, you can return to your own room."

"With Witch Girl," whispered Casey as she adjusted the pillow under DJ's leg and carefully pulled the blanket up over her.

DJ frowned then closed her eyes. She wanted to put in a nice word about Taylor, but she hurt too much. "I think I could use some pain meds about now."

"Good idea." Grandmother set the bag of prescriptions on the bedside table. "Casey, would you get DJ some water, please?"

Casey didn't seem to mind acting as the servant girl as she hurried off.

"I want you to know that, despite this inconvenience, I am proud of you for helping that little boy, Desiree."

With eyes still closed, DJ muttered "Thanks," and wondered who was more inconvenienced here—Grandmother or her? Not that it mattered.

"And while it's most unfortunate that you will not be able to practice for the fashion show with the other girls, I do expect you to come and observe at our lesson time. It won't be the same as participating, of course, but you can learn a few things by simply watching. And perhaps you'll be up and moving around in time for the fashion show."

DJ's eyes popped open. "You expect me to walk a runway with a broken leg and crutches?"

"The doctor said the surgery will make your leg almost as good as new before long, Desiree."

"But it's all bruised and nasty looking—and it hurts. Besides, I have cracked ribs too, remember."

"He said moving around will help the bones to heal. And, as you know, you are to report for physical therapy on Monday morning."

DJ let out a low groan as Casey set the water next to her.

"I know you don't feel too well just yet, Desiree; but in a day or two, I'm sure you'll be getting back to normal."

DJ didn't respond. How did a person respond to something like that?

"Get some rest, Desiree. Ring if you should need anything." Grandmother pointed to a small brass bell. "I told Inez to be on alert for you."

"Thanks," DJ muttered, relieved to see her grandmother leaving.

"Here," said Casey as she shook two pills into DJ's palm then handed her the glass of water.

"Thanks, but I'm not sure if two will be enough."

Casey chuckled. "Your grandmother doesn't let up much, does she?"

"Did you hear that she still expects me to be in the fashion show?"

Casey laughed louder. "Yeah. I think you should wear a miniskirt so that everyone can admire your lovely leg."

"She told me that I have to go to the training sessions and observe."

"Which start tomorrow afternoon," said Casey. "Gee, I can't wait."

DJ leaned her head back into the pillow and sighed. If a broken leg couldn't get her off the hook, nothing could.

"HOW are you feeling?" Inez asked DJ as she set a dinner tray on the small bedside table.

DJ pushed herself up on her elbows with a groan. "I've had better days."

"Sorry to wake you, but I thought you might be hungry. It's after seven."

"That's okay." DJ attempted to maneuver her broken leg over the side of the bed, but every movement seemed to spell pain—either in her ribs or her leg. In fact, she decided that she hurt all over. Kind of like she'd been run over by a truck.

"Need any help?"

"Just hand me the crutches, okay?"

Inez got the crutches then helped DJ stand. "I thought you would have a cast on your leg."

"Apparently that's not necessary when they put a metal rod in to hold the bone together." DJ took a tentative step toward the tiny bathroom that was part of this small bedroom setup.

"Metal!" Inez said. "Oh, now you will have trouble in airport security. My sister has a metal hip joint, and all the alarms go off when she tries to go through the metal detector."

"Something else to look forward to." DJ groaned again as she shuffled across the hardwood floor. Each step produced its own new form of pain.

"How do you like my room?" asked Inez as she held open the bathroom door.

"It's fine." DJ slowly moved past her. "Sorry you had to give it up for me."

"Not as sorry as I'll be tonight. Clara snores like a freight train."

DJ closed the door and sighed. Even everyday tasks like using the bathroom had become an enormous obstacle. What she really wanted was a nice long shower, but the idea of getting in there without help was overwhelming, and she wasn't about to ask Inez to assist her. After what seemed about an hour, DJ finally made her way out of the bathroom to see that Inez was still there.

"You didn't have to stay," said DJ as she slowly made her way across the room again, huffing and puffing with each painful movement.

"I wanted to be sure you didn't fall," she told DJ.

"Thanks." DJ sat down gratefully on the bed

Inez helped her get comfortable and then set the dinner tray on DJ's lap: "You all right now?" asked Inez as she paused by the door.

DJ nodded. "I'll be fine. The house seems quiet tonight."

"Most of the girls are gone."

"Gone?"

"It's Saturday night, Desiree. I guess they all have dates or something."

"Oh." DJ couldn't imagine that they all had dates, but perhaps they all had someplace to go. Rhiannon was probably at youth group, and Eliza was probably out with Harry. But DJ

64

wasn't sure where the others would be. For whatever reason, she felt left out. Not that she expected them to hover around her, but she had figured that someone would come down to visit.

DJ finished her dinner and managed to put the tray on the bedside table without too much pain. Then she leaned back into the pillows and sighed. She knew it was probably time for more pain pills, but she also knew they made her sleepy. It seemed like that was all she'd done all day. She wondered where Conner was and why he hadn't called or come to visit. But then she didn't see her cell phone anywhere, and he seldom called her on the landline.

She didn't want to feel sorry for herself, but it felt like everyone was out having a good time while she was stuck here in the housekeeper's room with no one to talk to and nothing to do. At least someone could've brought her a book. Or even a fashion magazine—there were plenty of those around.

"Hey?" called Taylor from the other side of the door. She opened it and stuck her head in. "You awake?"

"Yeah. Come in," said DJ.

"How's it going?" asked Taylor as she came in and peered down at DJ.

"You mean besides being in pain and bored as a gourd?"

"Sounds like you're having a great time." Taylor sat down in the straight-backed chair that was against the wall and glanced around the tiny room. "Nice little place you got here—kind of minimalist."

DJ nodded as she looked at the bare white walls. "I'm not sure if Inez stripped it down for me or if it's always like this."

"Maybe she had posters of hot guys all over the walls," said Taylor, "and didn't want you to get too excited."

DJ laughed then grimaced because it made her ribs hurt.

"You're really in bad shape, aren't you?"

"Ya think?"

"Do you need any pain medicine?"

"Probably, but it just knocks me out."

"If I were you, I'd be glad to be knocked out."

DJ nodded and sighed. "So, where is everyone tonight? Inez seems to think they all have dates."

Taylor chuckled. "Yeah, right. Let's see. Rhiannon went to her precious youth group thing. Eliza went out with Harry. And Kriti said she was doing something with her debate team friends—that sounds like loads of fun. And, oh yeah, Casey went out with Garrison. Since when have those two been a couple?"

"Since Friday." DJ frowned. "Was that only yesterday?"

"Well, since today is Saturday, yes." Taylor picked up DJ's prescription bottle and read the label. "Hmm. Vicodin. These as good as I've heard?"

"They're good for getting rid of the pain, but you better not take any of them." DJ gave Taylor a stern look.

Taylor set the bottle back down. "Hey, you missed yourself on TV tonight."

DJ rolled her eyes. "That's fine with me."

"I TiVo'ed it for you."

"I didn't know we had TiVo."

"That's because you don't. I do."

"Oh, well, thanks."

Taylor pushed a curly strand of hair off her forehead. "The Carter House girls have been getting a lot of local coverage lately."

"That's right. You made the news last week. And then me. I wonder who's next."

Taylor nodded. "Bonnie actually asked me to make a statement at the hospital too."

"About being missing?"

"Yeah. But I kind of evaded the question."

"What did you say?"

"Just that I had needed a little vacation. Then I talked about my heroic roommate and how much I admired her."

"You really said that on TV?"

Taylor snickered. "Yeah. And they bought it too."

"So, did they play it tonight?"

Taylor held up her chin and fluffed her hair as if she was posing. "Oh, yeah. And I must admit I look pretty good on camera too."

DJ could just imagine Taylor putting on a show for the camera crew. "What some people won't do for a few minutes of limelight," she said. But then Taylor always seemed to get more than her fair share of attention. Not that DJ envied her that. In a perfect world, DJ would avoid the limelight completely.

"So how long are you stuck down here in solitary confinement?"

"I guess until I can do the stairs. Not that I don't enjoy having a room to myself," she said quickly.

"Just don't get too used to it." Taylor winked. "So, will you be going to school on Monday?"

DJ considered this. The doctor had recommended three days of controlled moderate activity, and she was scheduled for physical therapy on Monday morning. "I don't think so," she said. "I need to get used to getting around on these crutches first."

"This is going to limit your shoe choices, you know."

"Yes. It's probably hard to look stylish hobbling around on crutches." Of course, this was something of a relief too. The pressure to "look good" all the time had taken a toll on DJ. Maybe her fashion-obsessed friends would cut her some slack now.

"Do you need anything?" asked Taylor as she stretched and stood.

"I'd like my cell phone," said DJ. "And something to read would be nice. And, if you don't mind, some more water."

"All righty then." She picked up the dinner tray and nodded. "Nurse Taylor at your service."

DJ tried not to look too surprised. This was a side of Taylor that most people never saw—a side that most people would never guess existed. After a few minutes, Taylor returned with DJ's cell phone, a book she'd been reading for English, a recent addition of *Vogue* (Taylor's fashion rag of choice), two bottles of water, and even one of the bouquets from the hospital, which she set on the straight-backed chair.

"I know that makes it a little crowded," she said, "but this room seriously needed some color."

"Thanks." DJ opened a bottle of water and took a swig.

"Oh, yeah," Taylor reached for something in her back pocket now. "I almost forgot. Hope it's not melting."

"Chocolate!" exclaimed DJ.

"From my private stash."

"Thanks!"

"Now, if you'll excuse me, I need a smoke."

DJ frowned. "I thought maybe you'd given that up."

Taylor looked exasperated. "Just because I'm being nice to you doesn't mean I'm applying for sainthood."

"Right." DJ opened her cell phone to see if Conner had called. And to her relief he had—three times.

"Tell him *hey* for me," said Taylor with a sexy voice followed by a wicked wink.

"Sure thing," said DJ, although she knew she wouldn't. Taylor had already made one move for Conner—fortunately Conner had not been interested. Still, DJ knew enough to know that no guys were completely safe when Taylor was on the prowl. Hopefully Taylor would keep her distance from Conner.

"Don't forget about the big modeling class today," said Casey as she moved DJ's breakfast tray from her bed to the table. It was Sunday morning, and DJ hadn't slept well after her pain meds had worn off in the middle of the night.

"Ugh, don't remind me," said DJ as she attempted to adjust the girdle-like bandage that wrapped around her ribcage. "Will you hand me my crutches, Casey."

Casey got the crutches then helped DJ out of bed. "Is it getting any easier—moving around I mean?"

"It wouldn't be so bad if my ribs didn't hurt so much." DJ took in a shallow breath. "In fact, *everything* hurts."

"Do you need any pain pills?"

DJ considered this. "What I really need is a shower. But maybe it would help if I took the pain pills first. I don't think I'll fall asleep in the shower."

So Casey gave her some pills, and DJ sat back down, waiting for them to kick in.

"Is it okay to get your incision wet?" asked Casey.

DJ explained about the superglue as she carefully peeled off the bandage.

"Seriously?" Casey shook her head as she looked at the incision running down the middle of DJ's shin. "That's so weird."

DJ frowned at the dark bruises on the side of her leg and the six-inch incision in front. It wasn't a pretty picture. "The surgeon said the scarring should be minimal, but I'm not so sure."

"Give it time."

DJ sighed and slowly stood, balancing herself on the crutches.

"Do you need any help in the shower?" asked Casey.

"I hate to admit it, but I think I probably do. Would you mind?"

"Nope." Casey chuckled as she followed DJ slowly making her way across the room. "And it won't be the first time I've seen you naked either."

"Well, just keep your comments to yourself."

But as Casey helped DJ peel off her tank shirt, she let out a slight gasp. "Man, DJ, you are black and blue."

DJ just nodded, blinking back tears from the pain. "Good thing I'm not into my looks, huh?"

Finally, Casey got the shower running at the right temperature, and DJ got in. "Don't go, okay?" she called from behind the plastic curtain.

"Don't worry, I'm sticking around."

The water actually hurt when it first began hitting her, but slowly it began to feel good, and DJ felt a faint rush of hope. Maybe she was going to get better after all.

"I feel like such a baby," said DJ as Casey wrapped a towel around her. "It's like I can't do anything for myself."

"Maybe it's good to accept a little help from your friends," said Casey as she toweled off DJ's hair.

"Maybe." DJ was remembering how Taylor had helped her last night. She considered mentioning this to Casey, but knew that it would probably just rub her the wrong way. "So things are really moving along with Garrison?" asked DJ as Casey helped put the girdle-like bandage back around her ribs. Casey had told her a little about their date last night. They'd seen the movie that DJ had wanted to see then gone out for a

Coke afterward. Not a big deal, but Casey seemed pretty excited. For Casey anyway.

"I guess."

"Meaning you're not that into him?"

"I don't know. I think I might be more into having a boyfriend, you know, than I am into Garrison. Still, he's nice. And maybe when you get to feeling better, we can go out with you and Conner. That'd be fun." Then Casey helped DJ dress and finally, feeling like she'd just run a marathon, DJ eased herself back into bed and closed her eyes. The pills were starting to work.

"I'll come wake you up in time for the modeling class," said Casey.

DJ's eyes popped open again. "Oh, that's okay, Casey. You don't have to." As in *hint-hint*. She'd rather just skip it.

"No, that's okay. It's *no* problem," said Casey, grinning.

"Thanks a lot." DJ closed her eyes again. It figured.

"HIPS FORWARD, CHEST OUT, shoulders straight, arms to the side," instructed Grandmother. "Relaxed but not slouchy, Casey!"

DJ was sitting on the couch, which had been pushed off to one side of the living room, creating "the runway" that began at the door and went up to the fireplace. Now the girls were taking turns walking and turning, and at the moment Grandmother was critiquing Casey.

"I've seen models who were slouchy," protested Casey.

"That was only for effect," said Grandmother sternly. "First they must learn to walk *correctly*. And *my* girls *will* walk correctly!" All Grandmother needed was a whip to crack.

Next came Eliza. She seemed to be getting the hang of it, even enjoying it. DJ could not imagine why. It looked like pure torture. And although she was hugely relieved not to be forced to physically partake in this exercise of the absurd, it wasn't easy to sit there either, remaining quiet as Grandmother coached the girls on how to walk. Good grief, hadn't they all been walking for quite some time now? It was humiliating.

"That's much better," said Grandmother as Eliza did her turn for the second time. "But not so much movement in your shoulders, dear. The motion comes from the hips." Now Grandmother took the makeshift runway. "Like this." And although she was almost four times their age, she actually made the walk look fairly effortless. Okay, it looked slightly ridiculous too, but it was amazing that someone her age could move like that.

"You see how it's done?" She cocked her head as she gracefully held out her wrinkled hands, all the while smiling confidently at the girls. And now, thanks to Eliza, they were actually clapping for her. Naturally, Grandmother ate that up, and DJ wondered what she'd ever done in life to deserve this.

"Taylor, your turn now." Grandmother stepped aside, watching as Taylor strolled through the living room like she was starring in Fashion Week.

"That's right," said Grandmother as Taylor turned when she reached the fireplace. "You girls pay close attention to Taylor. She's a natural. Taylor, why don't you do that again for the girls."

Of course, Taylor was happy to comply. Although you wouldn't know this by her expression, which was cool and reserved—yet full of confidence. How did she do it?

"See how relaxed Taylor looks." Grandmother was narrating her moves now. "See how her shoulders are squared, her hips are forward. Notice how one foot almost crosses the other and yet, she is so elegant and refined, so comfortable in her beautiful skin." Grandmother patted Taylor on the back when she reached the fireplace the second time. "Lovely, dear. Simply lovely."

Well, who wouldn't be comfortable in Taylor's skin? DJ let out an exasperated sigh and leaned back into the couch. Her ribs were starting to ache, and her leg was throbbing again.

She considered sneaking back to her room, but knew a graceful exit would be impossible with the crutches. Now Kriti was taking her turn. Poor Kriti. Next to the tall girls, she looked almost like a midget.

"Kriti, Kriti, Kriti …" Grandmother shook her head in scornful way. "We all know that you're short, dear, but you do not have to walk as if you're short. Hold your head high. Elongate that neck. Straighten your back. There, that's better. Stand proud, Little One."

DJ was surprised that these girls seemed more than willing to put themselves through this deprecating form of torture. Even Casey, despite her usual I-hate-fashion attitude, was being a pretty good sport as she made her second walk down the runway.

"That's better, Casey," said Grandmother as Casey made her turn. "You really are such a pretty girl. So much better since you removed those horrid safety pins from your face. But, still, I do wish you'd let your hair go back to its natural color. That black is so severe against your pale skin."

"I've seen other models who look just like that," said DJ from the couch.

"Yes, well, I've seen *plus*-sized models too," said Grandmother in a haughty tone. "That doesn't mean that I approve of *fat*."

Eliza giggled. DJ made a face but had the sense to control her tongue. Still, she was getting tired, and the pain in her leg was getting worse.

"Yes, yes, that's looking very nice, Rhiannon." Grandmother clapped her hands. "Now keep your palms toward you. Longer steps. Yes, that's better."

Finally, after all the girls had done several walks down the "runway," Grandmother seemed somewhat satisfied. But instead of letting them go, she began a lecture on the proper care of skin, hair, and nails. Not that Eliza or Taylor needed to be taught these things. Between the two of them, they probably had enough beauty products to open their own salon.

"There's nothing worse than having a model show up for a photo shoot with dirty hair and fingernails." Grandmother frowned with a disgusted expression. "And I've sent models away for not taking care with their complexions too. Oh, certainly, a small pimple can be airbrushed and dark shadows beneath the eyes can be adjusted, but if a girl doesn't care about her appearance, why should anyone else?"

DJ felt herself drifting as her grandmother droned on about chemically treated hair, split ends, and blemish control. It was like the woman was a walking, talking fashion encyclopedia. Hopefully there wouldn't be a test afterward.

Finally Grandmother was finished and dismissed the girls. "Remember," she said as they began to disperse, "next Saturday morning you will be fitted for the fashion show."

DJ almost asked if this included her, but she was afraid that her grandmother would say yes. It was better just to keep her mouth shut.

"This fashion show might be fun," said Eliza as the girls worked together to put the furnishings back where they belonged.

"Fun for some of you maybe," said Casey. "I'm not exactly looking forward to being gawked at by strangers."

"But at least it's for a good cause," said Rhiannon.

"Which good cause?" asked DJ as she slowly moved across the room. Her plan was to get to her temporary bedroom, take some pain meds, and then come back here and fall asleep watching TV.

"We don't know yet," admitted Eliza. "But, come on, girls, let's make it fun."

"Whatever you say, Pollyanna." Taylor rolled her eyes as she flopped down onto the couch, now back in place, and picked up the remote.

By the time DJ made it back to the living room, only Taylor was there. "Where'd everyone go?" asked DJ as she eased herself down into an easy chair, propping her leg on the ottoman.

"I guess I scared them away."

DJ frowned. "What did you do?"

"Just being my charming self." Taylor smiled innocently. "Hey, you want to see the news story I TiVo'ed?"

DJ agreed, then tried not to overreact when she saw her bruised and scraped face on the big screen. Good grief, if that's how she looked after Eliza's help, she couldn't imagine how nasty it would've been without it. Note to self, she thought, tell Eliza thank you.

"You look good," DJ told Taylor.

"Yes, I'm pretty photogenic," admitted Taylor. "And you would be too if you weren't so beat up."

When it was over Taylor flipped through the channels until she finally landed on an old forties musical with Doris Day. DJ thought it was kind of amusing that Taylor actually seemed to enjoy those unrealistic glamour movies, but she had no intention of mentioning this since she felt fairly certain that Taylor would take offense and turn it off. Besides, it wasn't long before all the singing and dancing combined with the Vicodin lulled DJ to sleep.

DJ woke up to a tickling sensation on her toes and the sound of giggles. She opened her eyes to see Eliza and Taylor hovering over her with Kriti and Casey looking on with interest.

"What's going on?" she asked, noticing that there seemed to be a whole lot of beauty products on the coffee table. Maybe Taylor and Eliza had decided to open a salon after all.

"We're practicing on you," said Eliza. "Now hold your feet still while I finish your toenail polish. And, seriously, DJ, when was the last time you had a pedicure?"

"Probably the time you helped me with it before."

"Well, your toes should be ashamed of themselves."

DJ looked down to see her toes painted a coral pink with little white things—were they tampons?—stuck in between.

Then she noticed that her face was feeling tingly. She reached her hand up to discover something smeared all over it. "What's this?" She examined what looked like green mucus on her fingers.

"It's a new kelp facial that my mom sent me," said Taylor. "I figured I'd try it out on you first. Just in case it makes your skin break out."

"It stings," said DJ.

"It's supposed to. It's exfoliating, and your skin should be smooth as silk when we're done."

"If it works, I want to be next," said Kriti as she rubbed a hand over her cheek.

"We decided you needed some special attention," said Eliza. "And since you were asleep—"

"And snoring," added Taylor.

"Yes, snoring rather loudly," said Eliza. "We thought we'd just go ahead and get started."

"I couldn't believe you slept through all that," said Casey.

"It's that pain medication," said DJ. She should be appreciative of this "special attention," but it was also a little humiliating to think they'd been working her over while she was asleep—and snoring! "It really knocks me out."

"Well, I've got homework to do," said Kriti as she paused in the doorway. "But let me know if that facial works."

"It needs to stay on for fifteen minutes," said Taylor as she wiped something else beneath DJ's eyes.

"I'm hungry," said DJ.

"Me too," said Casey. "Want me to go sneak something from the kitchen?"

DJ nodded. "Just don't get caught," she called as Casey slipped out.

"My work here is done," said Eliza as she dropped some things in a bag. "Just let those toenails dry for at least ten minutes before you move around." She blew an air kiss then made her exit. And, once again, it was just Taylor and DJ in the living room. Then the doorbell rang.

"Someone's at the door," said Taylor.

"Inez will get it," said DJ.

Taylor glanced toward the doorway. "I wonder who it is . . . maybe I'll check."

"Well, whoever it is, don't let them in here," warned DJ. She looked down at her strange-looking toes with her sweatpants rolled up to her knees. She didn't want anyone to see her like this.

"Back in a sec," called Taylor.

DJ's face was starting to sting even more now. Was it really supposed to feel like that? Or was this stuff burning her skin off? She was tempted to get up and go wash it off, but remembered about the toenails and then her broken leg. She was going nowhere.

"DJ's right in here," said Taylor in a sweet voice.

DJ sat up, turning in time to see Conner walking into the living room with a bouquet of pink roses.

DJ wanted to hide or scream or maybe even throw something. She glanced at the coffee table, wishing there was a baseball bat handy so she could clobber Taylor with it.

"Hey, good looking." Conner wasn't even trying to suppress a big grin as he set the roses on the coffee table. "Taylor told me that you were in the middle of a makeover. But I said I didn't mind."

"I tried to talk him out of it," said Taylor.

"I'll bet you did." DJ glared at her.

Taylor just shrugged. "Hey, he wanted to see you. Don't have a fit."

DJ leaned back into the chair with an exasperated sigh. "I think this is what they call 'insult to injury.'"

Conner laughed and sat down across from her. "I can leave if you want."

DJ actually *did* want him to leave, but it had been sweet of him to bring flowers. And it seemed rude to send him away so quickly.

"Make yourself at home," she said meekly. Then as he made an attempt at small talk, politely asking her about her leg and her ribs, she realized how juvenile she was acting. For a girl who claimed she didn't care about her looks, why should she freak over being seen like this? Still, she and Conner hadn't been going together that long ... and already he'd seen her at her worst—numerous times.

Finally, Taylor shoed Conner away, saying that she needed to remove the facial goop and that he should come back later, after DJ had a chance to get herself more together. Conner stood then smiled at DJ, but he actually seemed relieved to go.

"But I can't come back later," he told them. "It's my mom's birthday, and I promised my dad that I'd help him make dinner."

"What a sweet boy," said Taylor in a condescending tone.

"I think that's really nice," said DJ. "And thanks for coming by—and for the flowers. Sorry I was such a mess."

He chuckled. "That's okay. Are you going to be in school tomorrow?"

"Probably not."

"Well, I'll call you."

As soon as he left, Taylor began to remove the kelp goop from DJ's face. "I think we need to get you to the bathroom," said Taylor in a voice that sounded a little concerned.

"Is something wrong?" asked DJ as Taylor helped her up and gave her the crutches.

"I got food!" said Casey, bursting into the room with a tray in her hands. She started to set it on the table, but then she got an odd look. "What's wrong with DJ's face?"

"Nothing," said Taylor quickly. "We just need to get her to the bathroom to get this stuff off."

With their help, DJ moved as fast as she could, and when they got to the tiny bathroom, she peered at herself in the mirror to see that her face was lobster-red and puffy. She touched a hand to her cheek and looked at Taylor in horror. "What do I do?"

"Just rinse it with cool water," said Taylor.

So DJ began splashing cool water on her face. But each time she checked out her reflection, she could see it wasn't helping.

"I think it's supposed to be like that for a while," said Taylor. She handed DJ a towel. "I'll go get the cream that's supposed to follow the exfoliation. Maybe it will soothe this redness."

DJ just stared at her red face in horror. No way was she going to school tomorrow. For a moment she wondered if Taylor had done this on purpose, although Taylor had seemed nearly as rattled as DJ felt.

"Here," said Taylor as she reappeared with the cream. Now Casey and Eliza were standing behind her, all of them looking at DJ as if she were something from another planet, which she felt was a distinct possibility.

"Seriously," said DJ in a disgruntled tone. "With friends like you guys, who needs to get run over by a truck?"

"You mean an SUV," said Casey.

"Whatever."

They laughed, and Taylor assured DJ that her skin was going to be okay. But Grandmother was not a bit pleased when DJ came to dinner looking like she'd been in the sun too long.

"What on earth happened to you?" she demanded.

Taylor explained. And then, to everyone's surprise, she took the blame.

"Oh, well," said Grandmother, placated it seemed since it had been Taylor's mistake, not DJ's. "I'm sure she'll be fine. It's probably no different than a chemical peel. And since she's already incapacitated, it was probably a case of good timing." She smiled at DJ now. "I'm sure your complexion will look lovely in a day or two."

But when DJ got ready for bed, her face was still hot and irritated—which was a minor annoyance compared to the ache in her leg and the pain in her ribs every time she moved in the wrong way. She reached for her pain meds, but when she opened the little amber bottle, it was nearly empty. She poured the remaining pills into her palm—all six of them. How could this be? So she read the label and did the math to discover that, even after taking the full recommended dosage, there should've been more than twenty pills remaining.

Clearly, someone had helped herself to DJ's meds, and DJ felt fairly certain she knew who that someone was. If she weren't so sore and tired and if the stairs weren't such an obstacle with her crutches, she would go up there and confront Taylor right now. As it was, she would have to wait until morning.

9

Homecoming Queen

"I alreaDY TOLD YOU, DJ. I did *not* take your Vicodin." Taylor's voice sounded slightly bored now, as if she thought that would be more convincing. She had come to DJ's temporary quarters to check on DJ's face this morning, which was blessedly normal again, and then she'd acted all surprised when DJ had confronted her about the missing pain pills.

"Then why am I almost out?" demanded DJ. She shook the nearly empty bottle beneath Taylor's nose. "And you're the only one who showed the slightest bit of interest in them. Besides, I wouldn't put it past you, Taylor."

Taylor just smirked. "Well, you did seem to be enjoying the pills, DJ. Maybe you've been double-dosing."

"No, I haven't."

"Then someone else took them, DJ. Because, like I told you, I did not." She turned and walked out, slamming the door behind her. Despite Taylor's dramatic routine, DJ felt certain it had to be Taylor. She'd been in DJ's little "recovery" room a lot. She'd been the only one to mention the pills, acting like they were some kind of special treat. It just added up. It had to be Taylor.

DJ hobbled out on her crutches in time to see the girls leaving for school. Taylor left on her Vespa—probably ticked because DJ wasn't able to drive her and, naturally, Eliza wasn't offering. Plus, Eliza's car was already full. Well, it served Taylor right. And DJ didn't even care if it rained today, which looked like a possibility. Maybe another good soaking would help Taylor wake up.

DJ was tempted to tell her grandmother about the missing Vicodin—and about Taylor's other vices as well. What would Grandmother think if she knew that Taylor not only smoked and drank and engaged in casual sex, but stole prescription drugs as well? Still, DJ could just imagine Grandmother defending Taylor, reminding DJ of how "beautiful" Taylor was and what a future she might have in the fashion industry.

Besides, as much as DJ hated to admit it, and as irrational as it seemed, DJ still cared about Taylor. And since she'd been praying for the girl, she probably cared even more. Oh, sure, she didn't care for a lot of the stunts that Taylor pulled. And sometimes she almost wanted to kill Taylor. There was also something about this mixed-up girl that drew DJ in. And DJ had hopes that Taylor was changing. Okay, she was like a yo-yo, or a ping-pong ball, but she was changing. And yet, it was wrong for Taylor to steal DJ's pain meds. DJ knew that for a fact. Not only was it wrong; it was dangerous. And before the day was over, DJ intended to prove that Taylor was guilty.

"You seem to be getting around better," said Grandmother as Inez helped DJ back to a standing position with her crutches. To get down the front porch steps, DJ had to sit down on her bottom and ease herself down one at a time. Not exactly graceful, but better than taking a tumble.

"I guess," huffed DJ as she slowly made her way to Grandmother's Mercedes.

"You okay now?" asked Inez as she helped balance DJ, easing her into the front seat of the car.

DJ nodded. "Thanks."

"Maybe I should come with you," said Inez.

"No, thank you," said Grandmother briskly. "We'll be fine."

DJ's vote would be to let Inez come with them, but it was too late now. Inez closed the door, made a little wave, and Grandmother began to back up. DJ wondered how it was that she'd been so unlucky in family.

"Did you ever tell my dad about the accident?" asked DJ tentatively.

"No. Did you want me to tell him?" Grandmother glanced at DJ as she slowed for the stoplight.

DJ considered this. "No, not really."

"If you think he should know, you are certainly free to call him yourself, Desiree. But, as you know, I am not inclined to maintain a relationship with him." Grandmother sighed loudly. "When I think of how he treated my daughter, your mother, well, I find that it's unforgivable."

DJ nodded. The truth was that DJ found it unforgivable as well. Even as a Christian, she wasn't sure how to think about her father. Mostly she didn't. DJ decided not to think about him today either. Besides that, Grandmother was turning toward the hospital complex now.

Fortunately, the physical rehab building had a handy driveway for Grandmother to pull up and let DJ out. With a flat surface to walk on and electronic doors, DJ made her way inside without too much trouble and only the normal amount of pain.

She had just sat down to fill out the paperwork when Grandmother joined her, glancing around the medical facility as if it made her uncomfortable. Or maybe she was imagining that she was here for some kind of painful cosmetic treatment.

"I spoke to the receptionist," said Grandmother quietly. "She said your session will be nearly two hours, so I think I will go do some shopping." She smiled stiffly. "You don't need me to sit here and wait for you, do you?"

"No, of course, not."

"You have fun then."

DJ nodded and returned to the form. Fun. Yeah, right.

After a fairly long wait, DJ thought maybe she should have gone shopping too, but finally a slender brunette woman smiled down at her "Hi. You must be DJ. I'm Selena, your new best friend."

DJ smiled. "Are you my physical therapist?"

"I sure am. Are you ready for some hard work?"

"I guess so."

"Great. If you invest yourself in this, it will really speed up your recovery." Selena helped DJ stand up and led her to the therapy room. At first DJ was relieved to see what looked like regular workout machines, but as Selena put her through the paces, DJ realized that she was no longer the athlete she had so recently been. And two hours later, she was totally exhausted. Her entire body ached from the exercises, but she had to admit it felt good to be moving again.

"Here, let me help you get into your walking boot," Selena said kindly. "I may be tough in therapy, but therapy is over now and I can baby you." She grinned as she loosened the Velcro straps on the foam boot. "How's your pain level?"

"Everything still hurts a lot." DJ let out a groan as she slid her foot into the bright blue boot. "I've been taking my pain meds pretty steadily."

"That's okay," said Selena. "Part of recovering is to keep the pain at bay. It allows your body to relax and heal itself better."

DJ cringed as Selena adjusted the Velcro straps and then began to fasten them securely around the boot. "Too bad I'm almost out of Vicodin."

"Oh, didn't you have a full prescription?"

"I'm not sure. I mean, it seemed like I had more. And suddenly I didn't. The truth is, I think that my roommate might've taken some of the pills." The words popped out of DJ's mouth before she had a chance to consider whether or not to say them.

Selena looked at DJ with misgiving.

"I mean, I don't know for sure," DJ said. "But she's kind of like that."

"That's a serious charge, DJ."

"I know." She frowned. "What should I do?"

"Well, we'll get you another prescription. But you better make sure they're in a secure place — possibly a safe."

"Seriously?"

Selena nodded as she readjusted the top strap. "How's that feel?"

"It actually feels kind of good. Like it might support my leg better, and I won't feel so worried about bumping it or hurting it more."

"That's the main idea."

"So, am I actually supposed to actually walk on it?"

"Not yet. Just do some gentle pushes, the way I showed you. That kind of movement and pressure will help the bone to start knitting back together, and we'll increase it over time."

"How soon will I be able to walk on it?"

"If all goes well, like it seems to be, I'd think you could be putting some weight on it, along with your crutches, by late next week."

"And how long until I can lose the crutches?"

Selena looked up at the calendar—it was one from CCHS with a photo of the Mighty Maroons football team above it. She flipped it from September to October then pointed to the end of the first week. "We might have you walking with a cane by then." She grinned at DJ. "Hey, that would be in time for your big homecoming dance. You planning to go?"

DJ shrugged. "I don't know. Maybe."

"Well, I can't promise you'll be dancing, but maybe you could be crutch-free by then."

By the time DJ got home, she felt completely worn out. And, after a late lunch, she took a nap. When she woke up it was still a bit before three—before school got out. And she had a plan. She rang the little brass bell by her bed, and after a few minutes Inez showed up.

So far, Inez had been far more patient than usual, but now she looked slightly irate. "What is it?" she asked.

"Sorry to bother you," DJ said quickly, "but if you could help me, you could have your room back."

Now Inez brightened. "What do you need?"

"I just want to get my things upstairs, and if you could sort of hang around and make sure I don't fall, I'll try to make it up the stairs."

Inez looked slightly concerned. "Is that okay? Did the doctor say it's okay?"

"I practiced doing stairs at therapy today," said DJ. Okay, she didn't admit that it was only three stairs up and three stairs down. But at least she'd gotten comfortable with it. "And if you help me, I think I can do it."

"Okay." Inez nodded. "You tell me what to do, and I'll do it."

It took awhile, but eventually DJ, with Inez's supervision, made it up the stairs. Then, after Inez deposited DJ's things in her room and left, DJ began searching through Taylor's things, looking for the stolen pain pills. She was very careful, knowing that Taylor was pretty sharp when it came to her own things; but after about twenty minutes, DJ felt fairly certain that the pills weren't there. They were probably in Taylor's purse—or perhaps she'd already used them.

Whatever the case, DJ was determined not to allow this to happen again. And maybe she didn't have a safe to keep her Vicodin in, but she would find a safe place. She poured the pills into an athletic shortie sock, which she then turned inside its sock mate, making them into a sock ball, which was how she stored her socks. She placed this, along with her other socks, in her sock drawer. It looked perfectly normal. The only thing that made it stand out was the maroon stripes around the tops.

After that, DJ went into the bathroom and, enjoying the luxury of a nice bathroom with plenty of space, she decided to take a shower. Her confidence in getting around was growing, and she felt fairly certain that, keeping in mind some of the tips Selena had given her, she should be able to accomplish this. Although it took longer than she expected and she was completely worn out when she finished—so much so that she sat down on the bench in her bathrobe just to recover—it felt like a small success.

Sitting there, she heard someone coming into the bedroom. Probably Taylor. And, although the bathroom door was ajar, DJ didn't call out or say anything. She was just too tired.

"Hi, Mom," said Taylor in a flat-sounding voice. "I got your message and am finally calling you back. But it seems, as usual, you're not answering." Long pause now, and DJ wondered if she'd hung up, but then she continued. "Anyway, yes, I'm okay. No, I didn't kill myself. Yes, I considered it. And maybe I will follow through someday, but not today. And, no, there's nothing you can do to help me. Well, except send more money. It seems my expenses are greater than we thought. I guess that's all." Now it was silent again, and suddenly DJ felt like an eavesdropper. Well, actually she was. She nervously reached for a crutch and, in her haste, knocked them both onto the tile floor with a loud crash.

"Who's there?" shouted Taylor in a tough voice.

"It's just me," called DJ.

"What are you doing here?" demanded Taylor as she pushed open the door.

"Taking a shower."

"But why? Why are you upstairs?"

"I went to physical therapy." DJ tried to reach the closest crutch, but couldn't. "I learned stairs."

Taylor picked up the crutches and handed them to her. "Well, you could give a person some warning instead of sneaking around."

"I wasn't sneaking. I was just recovering from taking a shower. It was pretty exhausting."

Taylor pressed her lips together like she was thinking. Maybe she was going to confess to taking the pills. "Do you need any help?"

DJ considered this. "Actually, some assistance would be nice." So Taylor helped DJ put on the ribcage girdle then got her some clean clothes and finally helped her into her walking boot cast.

"You really are a mess, aren't you?" said Taylor as DJ finally got to her feet, arranging her crutches beneath her arms.

"Yeah, thanks for caring." DJ slowly made her way out of the bathroom and back to the bedroom, pausing to use her crutch to sweep her bed clear of the things that Taylor had tossed there. "I see you made yourself at home while I was gone."

"You don't have to be so grumpy." Taylor picked up a few more things and tossed them to her own bed. "I'm the one who should be mad at you."

"Why?" demanded DJ as she sat down on her bed with a loud sigh.

"For your accusation this morning."

DJ studied Taylor. "You still claim that you didn't take them?"

"It's the truth."

DJ kept looking at Taylor, and for some reason she thought maybe it really was the truth; but she wasn't convinced. "If it's the truth, you probably wouldn't refuse to let me see your purse." DJ nodded to Taylor's tan Chloe bag on the bed, the one she'd obviously taken to school today.

Taylor shrugged, reached for the bag, and tossed it onto DJ's bed. "Knock yourself out." Then she went into the bathroom.

DJ carefully searched the entire bag. And while she found cigarettes, condoms, fake ID, and several other condemning pieces of evidence against Taylor, there was no sign of the pills. DJ even checked an Advil bottle, but it contained only some red pills that looked like Advil. She zipped the bag and tossed it back to Taylor's bed.

"No luck?" asked Taylor as she emerged from the bathroom with an *Elle* magazine.

DJ looked carefully at her roommate. "You really didn't take them?"

"You know what, DJ," said Taylor as she sat on the window seat, neatly crossing one leg over the other. "If I really had taken those pills, and if you'd been that ticked at me for taking them, I probably would've just confessed and given them back to you. I mean, seriously, it's not really worth the fuss. If I needed Vicodin that badly, I would've figured out a better way to get it."

DJ nodded. Somehow she thought that was probably the truth.

"Besides, I think I know who took them." Without another word, Taylor picked up her bag and left the room. Well, whatever. DJ wasn't even sure she cared at the moment. Mostly she just wanted to take a pain pill and forget about all of it.

WOrn OUT FROM PHYSICAL THeraPy, moving back upstairs, taking that shower, plus being groggy from her pain
meds, DJ opted to remain upstairs. She'd already called downstairs to tell Clara not to set a place for her. Now she just needed
to find a way to have dinner brought to her room. DJ knew
Clara wouldn't want to do it herself since she hated going upstairs for anything, but maybe she'd send Inez up. Then, just
when DJ was about to give up, Casey and Rhiannon showed
up. Not only did they bring her food, but their own meals as
well.

"We thought we'd join you," Rhiannon said cheerfully.

"Unless you don't want us," said Casey.

"No, that'd be great."

"And if it's not too much trouble," said Rhiannon. "We'll set
dinner up in our room."

"So you can have a break from Taylor." Casey made her favorite witchlike impression, complete with claws and a snarly
smile.

"Give us a few minutes to set it up," said Rhiannon.

Ten minutes later, DJ made it to their room and saw that they had a little card table put between the two beds, complete with a table cloth and fresh flowers—one of the bouquets DJ got from the hospital—all set for her.

"It's like a party," said DJ happily.

"Here," said Rhiannon. "You can sit on my bed."

Casey scooted the table aside to make room for DJ to sit down.

"Wow." DJ set her crutches aside and rubbed her hands together as she looked at the meal.

Then Rhiannon bowed her head and asked a blessing.

"This was really sweet of you guys." DJ picked up her fork. "Thanks so much for thinking of me."

"To be honest, it was partially selfish. At least on my part," admitted Casey.

"Why's that?"

Rhiannon giggled. "I'm surprised Taylor didn't mention it already."

"What?"

"Homecoming queen nominations were made today." Casey rolled her eyes. "Both Eliza and Taylor made the final cut."

"And Kriti is going to be Eliza's campaign manager," added Rhiannon.

"And all those two can talk about is their big plan to get Eliza the crown—and money is NO object."

"Obviously." DJ hoped that Eliza didn't plan to actually buy her votes.

"Eliza already called Daddy Warbucks Wilton and asked him to give her a campaign budget." Casey just shook her head.

"And Kriti called her dad to see about getting some kind of giveaway things manufactured," added Rhiannon.

"So, this is serious then?"

"Oh, yeah. And guess who the third nominee was?" Casey waited.

"Who?"

"Madison Dormont."

DJ made a face. "Oh, this should be interesting, considering that Madison hates all of us."

"She's already started saying how it's wrong for a newcomer to win the crown—going on about how she was born in Crescent Cove, like fifty-something generations ago," said Casey.

"And, don't forget," added Rhiannon. "Madison's mother was homecoming queen back in the seventies."

"This should be interesting," said DJ. "But didn't you say that Taylor was nominated too?"

"Yes," said Rhiannon with wide eyes. "Can you believe it?"

DJ considered this. "Sort of."

"I mean, of course, she's a beautiful girl," said Rhiannon. "No one can dispute that, but I sort of thought, I mean, after that whole MySpace thing ... I thought it was kind of a shocker."

"It has to have been the guys," said Casey in a lowered voice, like she thought Taylor could've been outside the door eavesdropping. "I think they got together in the locker room and plotted the whole thing out. I seriously think she's getting the skanky vote."

"Do you think she'll win?" asked DJ.

"Who knows?" said Rhiannon.

"It's possible that the legitimate vote will be split between Eliza and Madison, and everyone else could vote for Taylor."

"Is Taylor taking this seriously? Do you think she'll actually campaign?"

Casey shrugged. "Who can tell with her?"

"Well, she didn't even mention it to me this afternoon," said DJ.

"You know Taylor." Rhiannon sighed. "She'll act like she doesn't care no matter which way it goes."

"Maybe," said Casey. "But I think she'll enjoy the attention in the meantime."

"How long *is* the meantime?"

"Two weeks," said Rhiannon.

"And I'll bet the meantime will get pretty *mean*," said Casey. And, even though the pun was lame, they all laughed.

"Are you going to school tomorrow?" asked Rhiannon as she and Casey stacked the empty plates together.

"I'm not sure," said DJ. "I mean, I want to get back—back to normal or whatever—but everything still hurts a lot. And I'm still taking the pain meds, which knock me out. It's not like I want to wake up in geometry with drool on my chin."

"Well, I picked up your homework and assignments," said Rhiannon. She went for her backpack.

"And I brought home your books," added Casey.

"Thanks, you guys." Then DJ made a face as they put a stack of papers and books on the bed next to her. "I guess."

"It's probably not as bad as it looks," said Rhiannon.

DJ sighed. "It's all kind of overwhelming. I mean, you finally feel like life is falling into some kind of normal, and then wham-bam, you get the rug ripped out from under you."

"That reminds me," said Rhiannon. "Josh Trundle, you know the editor of the school paper, well, he wanted to get a photo of you. He's doing an article about you for this week's paper."

DJ put the back of her hand against her forehead in a dramatic gesture. "Oh, the price of celebrity."

The girls laughed. Then Rhiannon said, "So, is it okay if he comes by after school tomorrow?"

"I'll be here with bells on," said DJ.

"Bells and casts and braces." Casey pointed to DJ's new walking cast. "How's that thing working for you? Can you walk yet?"

"Not yet. But my physical therapist said I can start putting gentle pressure on it, just to help the bone to mend."

"You should take up swimming," said Casey. "That's what I did when I sprained my ankle back in middle school. It really helped."

DJ considered this. "That's not a bad idea."

"Want me to check into it for you?" she offered.

"Sure. Thanks." DJ smiled at her friends. "What would I do without you guys?"

"Be tortured by Taylor," said Casey. "Seriously, I'm feeling guilty that Rhiannon and I kind of stuck you with her."

Rhiannon nodded. "Yes. Is it pretty horrible?"

DJ considered mentioning her missing pain meds, but then remembered how adamantly Taylor had denied being to blame. Also, she remembered Taylor's claim to know who the culprit was. "No," said DJ. "It's not that bad. In fact, Taylor is actually fairly nice to me."

"That's hard to believe," said Casey.

"Well, she should be nice to you," said Rhiannon.

"Yeah." Casey nodded with enthusiasm. "You're still a hero at school. All the volleyball team was asking about you, which reminds me." Casey grabbed her backpack again and pulled out a big envelope. "They all signed this for you."

DJ opened the envelope to find a get-well card as well as a gift certificate for $100 to Dan's Sporting Goods Shop. "Wow, that was nice of them."

"And Coach Jones said to tell you hey and that she hopes you're feeling better."

"I wish I could watch the game tomorrow," said DJ.

"Maybe you can." Casey shook her head in a dismal way. "Man, I just wish you could play. I can't believe the pressure on me now that the star player is gone."

"That's not true," said DJ. "You're just as good as I am."

"Maybe in your current condition."

DJ laughed. "Yeah, right."

"Seriously, the pressure is on. It's like the whole team expects me to hold everything together; and the harder I try, the worse it gets."

"You can only do what you can do," said DJ.

"I guess . . ." Casey sighed.

"So, do you really want to go to the game, DJ?" asked Rhiannon.

"It might be fun to see —"

"To see us lose?" Casey frowned.

Rhiannon laughed and turned to DJ. "I could drive you," she said. "I mean, if you trust me with your car. I do have my license, you know."

"Okay," said DJ. "It's a date."

"I'm sure the team will be glad to see you," said Casey.

"I hate to end the party," said Rhiannon. "But I do have homework."

"Looks like I do too," said DJ, glancing at the stack of assignments. "Although I suppose I can work on it during the day tomorrow."

Casey and Rhiannon helped DJ get her stuff back to her room. "Looks like the witch is in," whispered Casey, nodding to the closed bathroom where DJ felt pretty certain she could smell cigarette smoke slipping underneath.

"Hang in there," said Rhiannon.

DJ had just gotten settled on her bed when someone knocked on the door. "The door's open," she called.

"It's just little ol' us," said Eliza in that perky southern voice. "We missed you at dinner." Her brow creased with concern. "How're you doing today?"

"Just kind of worn out," said DJ. "I had physical therapy and then got myself upstairs and—"

"And we totally understand." Eliza grinned. "So, did you hear the big news?"

DJ glanced over to the still-closed bathroom door, as in *hint-hint, someone might be listening.* "Yeah. Congratulations. I hear you've been nominated for homecoming queen."

"And her chances of winning are really good," said Kriti with enthusiasm. "I heard lots of kids saying they had voted for her and that they like her lots better than Madison Dormont."

"Madison is a pain," admitted DJ.

"So . . ." Eliza smiled brightly. "We're hoping you'll want to help with the campaign."

DJ tried not to look too shocked. *"Help you?"*

"Well, we thought since you're kind of bedridden, well, maybe you'd have time to work on buttons or—"

"Fine thing," said Taylor as she emerged from the bathroom trailed by a cloud of blue smoke. "I barely step out of my room, and there's an invasion."

"Were you smoking in there?" demanded Kriti.

Taylor ignored the question, turning her attention to Eliza. "I can't believe your nerve."

"My nerve?" Eliza blinked innocently.

"Coming in here when my back is turned and trying to get *my* roommate to work on *your* campaign? That's takes some nerve."

"She might be *your* roommate, a matter she had little choice in, but she's *my* friend." Eliza placed her hand on DJ's shoulder in a possessive way.

Taylor scowled at DJ. "Are you going to put up with this?"

DJ didn't know what to say.

"It was my idea," said Kriti quickly, directing her words to DJ. "I thought we could make buttons with Eliza's photo on them. And I thought maybe you could help too—"

"You guys think that just because DJ is laid up with a broken leg and cracked ribs she has nothing better to do than make your stupid campaign buttons?" demanded Taylor as she opened the door and nodded toward it. "I think that's selfish and rude. And, in defense of my roommate, I am asking you to leave."

DJ was too stunned to say anything.

"Do you want us to leave, DJ?" asked Eliza.

DJ took in a slow breath. "Well, I am kind of tired tonight, Eliza. Can we discuss this another time?"

Eliza patted DJ's head. "Of course, sweetie, you get some rest. We'll talk later."

"And I forgot to mention that we'll give away chocolate with the buttons," said Kriti just before Taylor shut the door, practically in her face.

"That was a little rude," said DJ.

"I'll say," said Taylor, like DJ hadn't been talking about her.

"I meant you—shoving them out like that."

"Did you like being solicited to help make Eliza photo buttons?"

DJ smirked. "Well, not so much."

Taylor pointed at her. "See. I knew it. You and I are more alike than you are willing to admit."

DJ just rolled her eyes. "Whatever."

"So did you figure out who really took your Vicodin yet?"

DJ shrugged. "No."

"And you're not the least bit curious?"

DJ looked evenly at Taylor now. "Sure. Who do you think took it?"

"Casey."

DJ frowned. "Casey? Why would you think Casey?"

"I just know."

"How do you know?"

"Some things you just know, DJ. And I happen to know it was Casey who took your precious pills. It's not that big of a deal, really. I mean, not that I liked being blamed for something I didn't do, but it's not that surprising that Casey would take them."

DJ felt angry now. It was one thing for Taylor to deny taking the pills herself, and DJ mostly believed her, but to go around pointing the finger at someone else—well, that was just wrong.

11

HOMECOMING QUEEN

"SO, HOW DOES IT FEEL TO BE A HERO?" asked Josh Trundle. Josh adjusted his dark-rimmed glasses then opened a small black notebook. He was slightly nerdish, and DJ got the impression he was trying to imitate the guy who played Superman—when Superman wasn't so super. Or maybe she was thinking of the young assistant guy.

"I don't think of myself as a hero." DJ adjusted the pillow beneath her leg then leaned back onto her bed. It had seemed a little strange having a guy in her bedroom, but she'd been worn out from doing her rehab exercises and then practicing going up and down the stairs a few times with Inez supervising. And so she'd decided to stay up here for "the interview." Anyway, the door was open, and it wasn't exactly like she and Josh had any romantic intentions. If Grandmother happened to walk by, she'd probably just raise an eyebrow then continue on her merry way. As it was, the old woman was probably enjoying her "beauty rest."

"So." He actually licked the tip of his pencil. Ugh—did people really do that? Or was he just being theatric? "Tell me, in your own words, DJ, what happened on Friday afternoon."

DJ recounted the incidents leading up to and following her wild dive across the street to shove Jackson out of the way. "That's about it," she said finally.

"Let's back it up, okay?" He peered curiously at her. "What exactly was it, do you think, that made you happen to notice that the boy was in danger? And why do you think you were the only one to notice?"

She considered this. "Well, I guess it was probably a God thing."

He frowned. "A God thing? Can you please explain that?"

"I guess so. You see, I'm a Christian. I haven't been a Christian for very long so it's not like I'm really well versed in all this stuff. But it was like something inside of me—I mean like God—made me turn my head at just the right instant. And when I saw Jackson was in danger, I just took off. The vehicle was coming, and he was directly in front of it. I don't really remember exactly what happened, but somehow—probably with God's help—I managed to get across the street and shoved him to the curb."

"And that's when you got clobbered by the SUV?"

"Right."

"So, are you saying that God could show you that Jackson was in danger and that God could supernaturally empower you to shoot across the street—but that God couldn't protect you from getting run over?"

"I don't know." She thought about this. "I mean, I'm sure God can protect anyone from anything—I mean, since he's God and all."

"So, are you saying God didn't want to protect you?"

"I don't really know. Like I said, I'm kind of new at this. I don't have all the answers yet."

"But you think you will?"

104

"Well, no. I mean that sometimes you just have to trust God with things. At least that's what Rhiannon has told me."

"Like blind faith?"

She shrugged. "I'm not sure."

He asked a few more questions. "Well, I guess that's about it," he said as he closed his pad. "Oh, except for one more thing."

"What?"

"I hear that two of your friends are running for homecoming queen." He grinned. "Which one of them are you supporting?"

"Supporting?" DJ envisioned herself handing out money to Taylor and Eliza, which seemed pretty ridiculous considering they were both from wealthy families. Maybe she should ask them to support her.

"You know," he persisted. "Who will you be voting for?"

"Aren't the elections done by a secret ballot?"

He nodded.

"Well, then . . ."

"Point taken." He smiled and shook her hand. "It's been a pleasure getting to know you, DJ. I hope you get better soon. Will you be back at school this week?"

"I think maybe tomorrow or Wednesday. I'm trying to build up my strength."

"Thanks for taking the time to answer my questions." But as he gathered his things and exited her room, she felt like he'd left her with more questions than answers.

"Ready to go to the volleyball match?" asked Rhiannon shortly after Josh finished up.

"I guess . . ."

"Are you too tired?"

DJ hoisted herself to her feet now, getting her crutches into place. "No, I'm okay."

Rhiannon watched as DJ slowly maneuvered herself down the stairs. "Wow," she told her. "That's really good."

"I've been practicing."

Then Rhiannon helped DJ get into the passenger seat of the car, placing her crutches in the back. "You sure you trust my driving?" teased Rhiannon as she turned the key in the ignition. "I mean, I haven't driven since my mom left, you know."

"I'm sure you're fine," said DJ, but that was about all she said as Rhiannon drove them to school. DJ was still thinking about what Josh had said about God not protecting her. It was very unsettling. And what if it were true?

"You feeling okay, DJ?" asked Rhiannon as she pulled in front of the gym.

"Just thinking."

"Did Josh say something to you?" asked Rhiannon. "I mean about Haley."

"Haley?" DJ frowned. "Who's Haley?"

"Oh, nothing." Rhiannon hopped out of the car and got the crutches from the back, handing them to DJ.

But DJ didn't budge from the car. "Who's Haley? And why are you suddenly acting weird?"

"Haley Callahan," said Rhiannon with a slight frown. "She used to live here in town. She went to school with us. Her family moved right after our freshman year, and now they've moved back."

"So?" DJ peered curiously at Rhiannon.

"So, I don't know if Conner ever mentioned her to you before, but she used to be ... well, they used to ... you know ... they kind of liked each other."

DJ tried to wrap her head around this. "So, you mean this Haley girl used to be Conner's girlfriend? And now she's moved back?"

Rhiannon kind of smiled now. "I mean it's not like it's a big deal. I just thought you were being kind of quiet, like something was wrong, and I thought Josh might've said something. I'm sure he's known Haley and Conner since grade school and—"

"And you're worried that Conner might still be into her?" DJ pulled herself out of the car, balancing on her good leg as she got the crutches in place.

"No, not really. I just thought maybe you were."

"Well, I wasn't." DJ straightened her spine, holding her chin up. Why should she be worried? Conner was her boyfriend. He'd brought her pink roses.

"Great. So I'll park the car and see you in there."

"Okay." DJ made her way toward the gym, but once she got to the heavy glass doors, she realized she had a problem. Okay, maybe she had a lot of problems. But the problem at hand was how do you push open a heavy door without hurting yourself when you're on crutches? She looked around to see if anyone was nearby to help, but didn't see anyone. Then she noticed a door off to the side with a blue and white handicapped symbol on it. *Ah-ha*. But as she made her way to it, pushing the large button that caused the door to open automatically, a sadness washed over her. She, an athlete who had always taken real pride in her physical skills and abilities, was now disabled.

DJ stopped in her tracks. Was she really ready to watch her healthy teammates? To cheer them on from the bench? But then how would she explain herself? Why not just get this over with? With crutches moving as gracefully as she could, she hobbled into the gym, glancing around for a place to sit, when one of her team members spotted her.

"DJ!" the girl screamed, and soon the whole team was yelling and cheering—all for DJ! Casey was the only one who didn't come running over; she stayed back to continue her stretching. DJ thought maybe she even looked a bit impatient to start the game. But the rest of the team was slapping DJ on the back, which brought a jolt of pain with each hit, and giving her high fives until finally the ref wailed on the whistle, signaling the girls back to start the game. DJ sighed in relief. One more slap on the back, and she was going to scream.

"Sit here," Coach Jones commanded, patting the seat next to her.

"Thanks." DJ sat on the team bench, waving at Rhiannon to join them. Then the match started, and DJ tried to be a good sport by cheering for her teammates. But the same thought kept nagging at her. *I should be out there with them.* And, if she had been out there with them, they would probably be winning.

During the short break, after the CCHS team lost the first game, a short, stout blond man walked into the gym with Coach Jones's son, Jackson, with him. The little boy, still holding onto the man's hand, began to jump up and down, pointing with excitement toward DJ. Then the man let go of Jackson's hand, and he shot straight toward her. Good thing she wasn't on the other side of a busy street.

"Hey, Jackson." She leaned down to hug him, once again wincing from the pain. "How's it going, bud?"

He grinned. "Okay." Then he looked at her big blue walking boot. "How's your leg, DJ?"

"It's getting better."

He looked relieved. Then DJ introduced him to Rhiannon, and he asked if he could sit between the two of them to watch the game.

"Of course," said DJ, scooting over to make room.

"So this is our angel," said the man who'd accompanied Jackson into the gym after he had negotiated the crowd and made his way over. He squatted down to speak to DJ. "And

I am the negligent guy who let Jackson out of his sight last week."

DJ nodded. "Oh."

"Name's Rick Steele, and I'm your coach's boyfriend." He glanced at Coach. "Well, actually I'm still in the doghouse with her. I don't know where I'd be if you hadn't done what you did last week, DJ." He reached out his hand and firmly shook hers. "I am eternally grateful."

She sort of shrugged, suddenly uncomfortable with all this attention and gratitude. "I can't really take all the credit," she muttered. "It was kind of a God thing."

"Yeah, I have to agree with you there, DJ. I barely saw it myself, but it was one of those things that you never forget." He shook his head. "Really amazing."

"I'm just glad Jackson is okay."

"So am I." Then he frowned. "But, hey, I'm really sorry about you getting hurt like this. I've been trying to think of something I can do to show my gratitude."

She waved her hand. "Don't worry about it."

He stood and ruffled Jackson's hair. "Well, this little guy is pretty important to me. I'd claim him as my own kid if I could get away with it."

"Down in front," yelled someone behind DJ.

"Excuse me," Mr. Steele said quickly, moving to the end of the bench where there was a vacant spot. DJ was relieved to have that over with. He was a nice enough guy, but all the fuss over her just got overwhelming. Of course, seeing Jackson again was great—a good reminder that her pain hadn't been for nothing. Despite some news reporters, DJ felt certain that God really had used her to protect the little guy.

Finally the match was over, which the Mighty Maroons lost in a mighty way—just like Casey had predicted. And now

Rhiannon was chauffeuring DJ and Casey home. Of course, Casey was sulking in the back seat. She'd said only a few words since their team lost the last game … and consequently the match. DJ knew she was blaming herself.

"So, tell me about this Haley chick." DJ quietly directed this to Rhiannon.

"Who's Haley?" called Casey from the backseat.

"Oh, so you're still alive after all?" teased DJ.

"Just barely."

"Haley's a girl who used to live in town," began Rhiannon.

"*And* she used to be Conner's girlfriend," added DJ.

"Oh?" Casey sounded slightly more interested.

"Her family moved back here, and she started back at school yesterday," said Rhiannon.

"So what does that mean?" asked Casey. "I mean, just because she used to be Conner's girlfriend doesn't necessarily mean he's still into her, right?"

"Absolutely." Rhiannon nodded her head firmly.

"Has Conner mentioned her to you, DJ?" asked Casey.

"No." DJ tried to remember their phone conversation last night. It had been kind of subdued, but she thought it was probably her fault since she'd just taken a pain pill before he'd called.

"Oh, yeah," said Casey. "Before I forget, I mentioned to Coach Jones that you were thinking about swimming, DJ. So she called over to the pool and set it up for you. Now you can swim laps with the swim team."

"With the swim team?" DJ frowned.

"Not as a member of the team, of course, but she's going to fix it so that you can have access to the pool when they are there. She said that'll be a great way for you to get into shape for soccer."

"Soccer." DJ sighed. Would she ever really be able to run, jump, or kick again? Right now, especially with her leg and ribs aching with each bump in the road, it seemed like the impossible dream.

"HOW'S HaLEY?" DJ was propped up in her bed with her cell phone to her ear. She and Conner had been talking for about half an hour, when DJ sensed their conversation was about to end. But she wasn't ready to say good-bye. Although she hadn't meant for her question to sound like an accusation. As soon as the words came out of her mouth, she wanted to reel them back.

"How did you hear about Haley?" asked Conner.

"Rhiannon told me about her," said DJ in what she hoped was a cheerful and natural-sounding tone. "She sounds nice, Conner. I'll bet you're glad she's moved back to town."

There was a long pause. "Well, yeah. We were pretty good friends."

DJ made a little laugh. At least that's what she wanted it to sound like. "Hey, I heard you were more than just friends."

He cleared his throat. "Yeah, I guess."

"You can be honest with me, Conner. You must've really liked her, right? It's not like you need to hide anything."

"Yeah, I liked her. But it was probably a kind of a puppy love thing. You know? I mean, she was the first girl I'd ever had a crush on."

113

"Did you kiss her?" Okay, as soon as this was out, DJ wanted to grab it back. Why was she being so nosey? Talk about insecure!

There was another long pause before he finally he said, "Uh-huh."

"Sorry," she said quickly. "It's not like it's any of my business."

"That's okay," he told her. "It just seems like a really long time ago. And, honestly, DJ, I hardly ever think about her anymore."

Meaning he used to think about her all the time?

"So, don't worry about it, okay?" he continued. "And I hope you can meet her. I think you'll like her. She's into sports too. And she's smart and just a lot of fun."

"Great," said DJ with absolutely no real enthusiasm. "I can't wait."

"So, when are you coming back to school?"

DJ considered this. "Well, I have a two-hour physical therapy appointment tomorrow, so I think I'll probably be kind of worn out. Maybe I'll come on Thursday."

"We have a soccer match on Thursday afternoon, on the home field. Come, if you feel up to it. I hear the weather is supposed to be good."

"Sounds fun," she said with genuine enthusiasm. "I'd love to come."

"Great. But I'd better get to homework now."

They said good night and hung up. But as she closed her cell phone, DJ had an uncomfortable feeling deep inside. And she felt pretty sure that it was related to Haley Callahan. She knew that it was wrong to hate someone—especially someone you hadn't even met—but what she felt toward this unknown girl wasn't exactly Christian love.

"Trouble in paradise?" asked Taylor.

DJ jumped and turned to see Taylor emerging from the bathroom. She hadn't even known that Taylor was upstairs. The bathroom door had been open, and Taylor usually firmly closed it when she was in there. Had she been listening to the whole conversation?

"What do you mean?" asked DJ.

"I mean *his girlfriend's back and she's gonna make you sorry*—hey, la, hey, la—*his girlfriend's back.*" It just figured that Taylor knew some stupid old song to go with a time like this. And, naturally, she sang it beautifully too.

DJ threw a pillow at her and scowled.

"Sorry," said Taylor as she plopped onto her bed. "I should probably have more compassion for the invalid girl."

"Why are you so mean?" demanded DJ.

Taylor shrugged. "I guess I just can't help myself."

DJ leaned back into the pillows and opened her history book, pretending to be reading.

"Have you seen her yet?"

DJ pretended to be so obsessed with the Reconstruction period that she hadn't heard Taylor.

"She's in art with me and Rhiannon," continued Taylor. "It seems like she and Rhiannon are old buddies."

DJ glanced over the top of the book. Seeing that Taylor was watching her, she turned the page.

"I know you're not really reading," said Taylor. "And I also know that you're dying to know more about this girl."

DJ slammed the heavy book closed and glared at Taylor. "And it seems that you're determined to tell me about her." She folded her arms across her chest and waited.

Taylor just smiled, in her catty sort of way, as she slowly opened a bottle of nail polish and bent over to touch up her toenails.

DJ knew this was a game. She knew Taylor wanted DJ to beg. But DJ just didn't want to play. So she opened her book again, and this time she actually did begin to focus on what it took to rebuild the United States after the Civil War.

"Fine," said Taylor as she set the nail polish jar on the bed-side table with a clink. "I'll tell you anyway."

DJ glanced up with a blank look. "Huh?"

"Haley is kind of a shrimp. Barely over five feet tall, although she wears heels—and actually has pretty good taste in shoes. She's really petite. I'm guessing she barely weighs 100 pounds soaking wet. She's got short dark hair and these big brown eyes and a pixie-like nose. Kind of Audrey Hepburn looking."

Okay, DJ knew that was a high compliment since Taylor really admired Audrey Hepburn. But DJ just shrugged, like no big deal.

"And she's nice."

DJ felt her eyebrows lift. "So, what exactly does that mean, Taylor? I mean, coming from you—how do *you* define nice?"

"She's friendly. And not full of herself or stuck-up or ridiculous."

DJ nodded. "Okay."

"Kind of like you." Taylor gave DJ a smirky smile.

"Is that supposed to be a compliment?"

"Take it or leave it." Taylor hopped off her bed and went back into the bathroom. This time she closed the door.

So now, as DJ attempted to refocus her attention on the Reconstruction period, she was stuck with this image of a cute little brunette girl who was Conner's first crush. And she was "nice." Just great!

"Hey, you're doing better," said Selena as DJ finished a fairly graceful set of stairs during her physical therapy session.

"Thanks." The truth was DJ was determined to get better. And fast. It was only Wednesday, but with Conner's ex-girlfriend on the prowl, DJ needed to be able to walk to keep up. In fact, she might even need to run. "Hey, I've got a question for you, Selena," said DJ as she slowly pushed the bench press forward again. It was set at "sissy" weight and yet DJ was sweating and in pain.

"What is it?" asked Selena.

"My volleyball coach has worked it out for me to swim laps with the swim team," said DJ as she breathlessly let the press come down. "Not competitively, of course. Should I go for it?"

"Of course." Selena smiled. "That's great. There's hardly a better strengthening exercise than swimming."

"Yeah, but it means I have to put on a swimsuit."

Selena laughed. "Well, I can tell you probably look pretty great in a swimsuit, DJ. No worries there."

"So, do you think I should get started on it this week?" asked DJ.

"Sure. Just be careful getting in and out of the pool." Selena glanced over to one of the exercise stations. "In fact, we should work on how you do that, okay?"

So they worked on it, and DJ realized that it was going to be awkward, not just with her leg, but the ribs made it tricky too. After a while, she sort of got the hang of getting up and down the short ladder without too much pain.

"The main thing is to not reinjure yourself," said Selena as they finished with some stretches. "And I know you're eager to get back to normal, but it just takes time."

DJ nodded, trying to look positive. But mostly she felt discouraged. It was so strange having a body that no longer responded to her brain. She had always been so active—sports and movement had been a huge part of her life. And now she was like an old person. Or, like Taylor enjoyed saying, "the invalid girl."

"Are you okay?" asked Selena.

DJ blinked. "Oh, yeah. I was probably just feeling sorry for myself."

"That's not uncommon." Selena seemed to be considering something. "But if you want to be cheered up, I know someone who could—"

"No, no," said DJ quickly. "I'm fine, really." It was one thing to undergo physical therapy, but DJ would draw the line at seeing a shrink.

"Okay. But if you change your mind. I have a friend who—"

"No, thanks. Really, I'm fine." DJ glanced at the big clock then reached for her crutches. "And I'll bet my grandmother is here. I should probably get moving."

Grandmother wasn't waiting though, and DJ had to sit around for half an hour before she finally showed up. Grandmother offered an apology of sorts, and DJ just nodded and climbed into the car. Mostly she just wanted to get home.

But once she was home, DJ didn't know what to do with herself. She felt slightly lost in the large, quiet house. As usual, Grandmother took her lunch in her room, and DJ sat by herself at the big dining table. Then she hobbled around the house and finally went upstairs to finish up her schoolwork, which didn't take that long. She took a short nap, and when she woke up, it wasn't even three o'clock.

If she were in school, she'd be in PE right now. DJ thought about how she and Taylor usually had a friendly competition in whatever it was they were doing because, despite Taylor's claims of not liking to get sweaty, she was good at most sports. In fact, it was the Varsity girls' volleyball team's loss that Taylor refused to go out for it.

DJ thought about going to the pool this afternoon, but knew that she wasn't ready to drive yet. Selena had said that she would probably be okay by next week. It helped that DJ's right leg was fine and that her car was an automatic.

She had to get out of this house. She called Eliza's number and, to her surprise, Eliza answered.

"Oh? I didn't think you'd have your phone on," DJ said quickly. "I was just going to leave a message."

"That's okay," said Eliza quietly. "I was just taking something to the office for Mr. Dewitt. What's up?"

"I feel like I'm going crazy, stuck in this house."

"Well, I can't give you a ride," said Eliza. "Kriti and I are working on some things for my campaign."

DJ sighed. "Oh, the big campaign . . ."

"Hey, it may seem like nothing to you, DJ, but I really want this."

"Yeah. I know."

"But how about if I ask Rhiannon? Maybe she could run home and give you a ride to the pool. I could even let her use my car. How's that?"

"Thanks." DJ brightened. "I really do appreciate it."

"I'll tell Rhiannon to call you to confirm it, okay?"

"Okay."

"And maybe you'll consider supporting my campaign now?"

DJ laughed. "I'll think about it."

"Great. Because you are still quite a celebrity around here."

DJ sighed as she looked down at her big fat blue walking boot. "Yeah, I feel so totally famous."

Rhiannon was pleased to borrow Eliza's little Porsche and pick up DJ. "This car is so hot," said Rhiannon as she drove, perhaps a little too fast, back across town toward the community pool that the high school used for the swim team.

"You better be careful," warned DJ. "You don't want a ticket—or worse yet, a wreck. I mean, look what happened to me."

"Right, but you leaped in front of an SUV."

"I'm just saying."

Rhiannon hopped out and got DJ's crutches for her, helping her to put on her backpack, which contained DJ's towel and swimsuit.

"What time should I pick you up?"

DJ considered this. "Like an hour, do you think?"

"Sounds good to me. How about 4:30 then?"

"Great."

"Call me if you need me sooner." Rhiannon frowned. "Or I can stick around if you want. Although Eliza did coerce me into helping them with their little sign-making project."

"No, I'm fine." DJ smiled. "You go help our dear Eliza."

"Even if it makes Taylor mad?"

DJ shrugged. "Do what you think is right."

"Be careful," called Rhiannon as DJ made her way up the cement steps that led to the pool's entrance. DJ just nodded, focusing her attention on each step. The whole crutches thing would probably have been a lot easier without her ribs to contend with. As it was, DJ felt seriously challenged. But finally she was in the dressing room. Fortunately, it appeared that the swim team girls had already been there and, judging by the noise, were just getting ready for their practice.

DJ went into one of the few dressing rooms, something she wouldn't have done before the accident. But she knew that getting dressed and undressed wasn't exactly easy anymore. And she didn't want anyone to see her struggling. It took about ten minutes, but finally she had her old one-piece suit pulled on. Now she felt seriously tired and wondered if she even wanted to swim. But she'd gotten this far, and she wasn't ready to give up.

She got her crutches into place and realized that she needed to be extremely careful on the wet surfaces. Not only would a fall be embarrassing, it would seriously hurt. So, feeling like she was about 100 years old, she very slowly and cautiously made it out to the edge of the pool—near what appeared to be an unused lane. The swim team swimmers looked like predatory sharks as they chopped and splashed through the other lanes. She hoped they were too busy to notice "the handicapped girl"—since DJ felt she was moving at the speed of an unmotivated slug as she made her way across the deck.

"Need any help there?" asked a lifeguard seated on the lookout chair.

"I'm okay." She glanced up nervously, curious as to whether she knew this guy or not. He was good-looking, but not familiar. "But can I leave my crutches here by the side of the pool?"

"I better stick them out of the way." He hopped down and waited as she worked her way closer to the edge. "Just yell when you need 'em."

"This is the first time I've done this," she said as she handed him the crutches and reached for the top of the pool ladder to balance herself.

"Hey, you're the girl who saved Coach Jones's son, aren't you?"

She smiled at him and nodded.

"Well, nice to meet you. How's your leg doing?"

She grimaced. "At the moment it's hurting." She touched her ribcage, now free from the usually constrictive, but supportive brace. "And so are my ribs. Man, I hope I can do this without drowning."

"I'll keep my eye on you," he promised.

DJ slowly lowered herself to a seated position. Everything ached.

"Just take it easy," he said, bending down in a reassuring way. He had short brown hair, slightly bleached by sun and chlorine, and clear blue eyes. In a way he reminded her of Conner, except he was probably even better looking. Not that she'd admit that to anyone. Or perhaps it was simply that he was being so kind to her.

"Looking good," he said as she held onto the ladder and slowly eased herself down into the water.

She took in a sharp breath, partly from the cold water and partly from the pain.

"You okay?" he asked, his face down low and close to hers.

She nodded. "Just kind of aching."

"Kind of like you got run over by a truck?" His blue eyes twinkled.

"Kind of like that."

He gently patted her on the head. "Just go easy, DJ."

She nodded, trying to acclimate to the water temperature. "You know my name, but I don't know yours."

"Caleb Bennett." He grinned. "At your service."

"Thanks." She pushed off and carefully began treading water. The motion on her left leg was pretty painful, so she mostly used her right one. "Hopefully I won't need rescuing."

"Well, if you do, I'm your man." He winked and stood, and DJ slowly took off in a somewhat lame sidestroke. Now if she could only make it to the other side of the pool without assistance.

"WAY TO GO, HALEY!" yelled the swim team coach from the other side of the pool. He'd been yelling a lot, but this time he got DJ's attention. It was her third lap, really one and a half laps since you had to go back and forth to equal one full lap. But when you're in pain you count things differently. Still, she thought he had said "Haley," and DJ wondered if that could possibly be Conner's Haley. Okay, she wasn't Conner's Haley anymore.

At least DJ hoped not.

She looked over to where the swim coach was showing a petite dark-haired girl a chart and holding out a stopwatch for her to see. The pretty girl simply nodded and smiled. She then took her position on a starter box, dove perfectly back into the pool, and effortlessly cut through the water. Even though DJ was halfway across the pool, this girl easily caught her, passed her, turned, and passed her again. Almost in the same place. Of course, this girl didn't even glance in DJ's direction. Why should she? And yet DJ felt she couldn't take her eyes off the girl. That had to be Haley Callahan.

After a while, Haley made her way to the diving pool where diving practice was just beginning. DJ was at the far edge of her lap lane by now, clinging to the side and watching as Haley scaled the high-dive ladder then, barely pausing to compose herself, performed a stunning backward-flip-with-a-twist kind of dive, slicing through the water with barely a splash. When she surfaced, her teammates were all clapping and cheering.

"This is so unfair," yelled a gangly redheaded girl. "Haley Callahan's first day at practice and she makes the rest of us look like total losers."

"Hey, just be glad she got here before the season ended," said a guy. "We might actually have a chance at the finals now."

DJ turned and swam very slowly back to the other side of the pool. She'd seen enough. And she'd swam enough. She felt tired and sore.

She was slowly working her way up the ladder when she noticed that Caleb was standing above her with her crutches in hand. Then he actually stretched out his forearm toward her. "Want to grab on?"

She gratefully grasped his arm with both hands, and he easily lifted her as she hopped on her good leg, up the ladder and out of the water.

"Thanks," she gasped as he helped her with her crutches. "I'm not even sure I could've done that without you."

"Well, you're doing great for your first time, DJ. Just be careful on the wet deck." Then he actually walked her to the dressing room door.

"Thanks, Caleb."

"You take it easy, okay?"

"Okay." She paused to catch her breath.

"And maybe I'll be seeing you around this place. I work on Monday, Wednesday, and Friday—from three until closing."

She wondered if this was some kind of a hint. "Do you go to our school? I mean CCHS?"

He chuckled. "Well, I *used* to. I graduated a couple years ago. I'm in college now. I'm trying to save up enough money to transfer to Yale by next spring."

"Yale?"

He shrugged. "Yeah. It's not that big of a deal."

"It's impressive to me."

"It'll be more impressive once I'm actually there." Then he grinned. "But it was fun being accepted."

She nodded. "Well, thanks again for the help." Then she slowly made her way to the showers. The warm water felt good, and she took her time soaping up; finally, since no one else was around and she could balance herself on the shower handles, she managed to peel off her wet suit and rinse it out. Then she tied it around one of her crutches, and feeling rather proud of this achievement, she shampooed her hair and was just getting her crutches in place when the sounds of girls' voices began coming into the locker room. *Okay*, she told herself, *this is no big deal.* She'd been involved in sports for ages, and girls seeing girls naked was no big deal. Except that her body was still black and blue with bruises and her incision was kind of purplish and she could barely move.

Still, she knew she couldn't hurry. But as the girls came into the shower area, their voices grew instantly quiet. Although her back was to them as she was hobbling toward the dressing area, she knew they were staring at her. Perhaps even pointing, nodding, and trying not to laugh.

"That's DJ Lane," said one of them, "the girl who rescued Coach Jones's little boy."

"Hey everyone," DJ said, still moving slowly. "I just came for some physical therapy." Just then her swimsuit slipped off her crutch, but before she could pick it up, someone else did.

"Here you go," said the petite dark-haired girl, tying it around the crutch again. "I'm Haley Callahan."

DJ nodded, feeling totally embarrassed now. Good grief—could it be she was standing here totally naked, bruised up and on crutches, meeting Conner's old girlfriend? Could it possibly get worse? "Thanks. I'm DJ."

"Everyone knows who you are," called out another girl.

"And we think what you did was very cool," said someone else.

"Thanks." DJ sighed and slowly began moving back toward the dressing room. Okay, it wasn't that bad. But not something she particularly cared to endure again.

"Yell if you need any help," said Haley.

"Thanks." But even as she said this, DJ knew that she wouldn't. She made her way back to the dressing room where her things were still on the bench. She hadn't even thought of using a locker. Oh, well, fortunately they were still there.

Of course, it took her even longer this time. First she had to dry off. Then she had to get on her rib brace, and it kept sticking to her damp skin. Finally she had herself mostly back together, except for her backpack. Not only was it too tight in the tiny cubicle, but her coordination was being challenged by pain and exhaustion.

Using a crutch to slide open the curtain, she hobbled out, pushing the backpack in front of her. Maybe she'd just leave it and see if Rhiannon could get it for her.

"Looks like you need some help," said Haley. She was completely dressed now, her hair was dry and in place, and she even had on a little bit of makeup. In fact, she looked just about perfect.

DJ sighed. "Yeah, I think so. This backpack thing is a pain."

Haley slung her own bag over a shoulder then picked up the pack. "Why don't I carry it for you. Do you have a ride coming?"

DJ nodded as she moved toward the door. "Rhiannon Farley."

"Oh, I know Rhiannon."

"I know, and you know Conner too."

Haley laughed. "Oh, did he tell you about us?"

DJ glanced at her.

"I mean, how we were all in love back in middle school?" She laughed louder now, and as much as DJ hated to admit it, this girl had a great laugh. The kind of laugh that made you want to laugh too. "And how I was all brokenhearted when my dad's job got transferred and we moved to Indianapolis? I just knew my life was over—and then after a week or so I was in love with a totally different guy named Blake."

Despite herself, DJ was smiling now. "No, he didn't tell me all that."

"Well, don't worry, DJ. I'm not putting the moves on your boyfriend."

"I didn't really think you were. But I'll admit I've been feeling a little out of things. It's so hard being, well, as my roommate says, 'the invalid girl.'"

"But you're getting around pretty well," pointed out Haley.

"I guess." They were outside now, and DJ saw Eliza's Porsche coming toward them. "Well, there's my ride."

"Nice ride," said Haley. "Is that Rhiannon's car?"

"No. Eliza's."

"And you girls all live in the same house?"

DJ carefully made her way down the steps. "Yeah, it's pretty weird. It was my grandmother's idea."

"And she used to be the editor of some big fashion magazine?"

"Sounds like you've done your homework."

"Well, the word gets around." Haley opened the passenger door, and Rhiannon blinked in surprise as Haley greeted her and then helped DJ get situated in the seat.

"Thanks," said DJ. "It was nice to meet you."

"Let me know if you ever need a ride to the pool," said Haley. "I drive over every day after school; well, unless I go to morning practice, but that takes real discipline."

"Thanks, I'll keep that in mind."

Haley waved then shut the door, and DJ turned to Rhiannon and grinned. "She *is* nice."

"That's what we tried to tell you."

"Is she a Christian?"

Rhiannon nodded as she pulled out. "Yep. I actually asked her about it today. She was wearing a silver cross, and I figured that was sort of like an invitation. She's been a Christian for a couple of years. Cool, huh?"

"Yeah. And, man, you should've seen her diving today. She's really good."

"Apparently she's even better at gymnastics," said Rhiannon. "I mean, she used to be pretty good, but I hear she's really taken it up a few notches."

"I can imagine that."

"Did she say anything about Conner?" Rhiannon's voice sounded uneasy now. Like she was worried.

"Just that it was over." Then DJ replayed how shattered Haley had been, but how she'd quickly found a new crush.

"Well, that's good to know," said Rhiannon.

"So, how did the sign making go?"

"Pretty well. Eliza already has a little fan club that's helping. Mostly I just outlined the signs, and they were all doing the rest of the work."

"She's really into this homecoming queen thing, isn't she?"

"You got that right."

"Hasn't she ever seen Steven King's movie *Carrie*?"

"I don't know. What's it about?"

"You haven't seen it? It's like a classic. Hey, maybe we should rent it and force Taylor and Eliza to watch it."

"Is it scary?"

"Duh? It's Steven King. Although to be honest, I didn't even get to watch the whole thing. All I know is that this girl gets pig's blood dumped on her at the homecoming dance as a cruel joke. I was about twelve when it was on TV one night. My mom caught me watching it and turned it off."

Rhiannon laughed. "Smart mom."

DJ sighed. "Yeah, she was." In fact, although DJ had complained loudly, she had been secretly relieved when Mom turned off the movie. It had been a little outside her comfort zone. All she really remembered was that the poor girl was picked for homecoming queen as a mean joke. And everyone knew that wasn't the case with Eliza and Taylor. At least DJ didn't think so.

"YOU LOOK BEAT, DJ," said Casey as she passed the salad dressing. DJ had considered taking her meal upstairs tonight, but didn't want to aggravate Clara or make a fuss. Still, she looked forward to calling it a day.

"I am pretty worn out," admitted DJ.

"Hopefully you're not too tired to help us with some things for Eliza's campaign tonight?" said Kriti. "We're having a work party here at the house. Mrs. Carter said it was okay."

"Why should DJ help *you?*" asked Taylor in an irritated tone.

"Why shouldn't she?" asked Eliza. She smiled sweetly at DJ. "After all, I did let Rhiannon use my car to chauffer you around, didn't I?"

"You did." DJ poured runny low-fat dressing on her green salad and looked up at Eliza. "And thank you for that. But it really wasn't meant to be a bribe, was it, Eliza? Surely you're not running your campaign like that, are you?"

Eliza smiled innocently. "No, no, of course not. I just got the impression that you were going to support me in this, DJ."

"Why should she?" demanded Taylor.

Grandmother cleared her throat rather loudly. "Girls, girls. Now, I do hope you won't allow the homecoming queen competition to divide our happy little family. I happen to think it's wonderful that two of our girls are competing for the crown. Such an honor. And, oh my, the fashion show committee was so pleased when I told them about it at lunch yesterday. Louise Bristow even reminded me that Desiree's mother was once crowned homecoming queen."

"Seriously?" DJ stared skeptically at her grandmother. "I've never heard that before."

Grandmother waved her hand. "Oh, you know how your mother was. She never liked that sort of attention."

"What year was it?" asked Rhiannon. "Maybe we can find the old photos in the school archives."

Grandmother considered this. "Well, it must've been nearly thirty years ago. I was in New York, but someone sent me the newspaper photo."

"You missed seeing your daughter crowned homecoming queen?" asked Eliza.

Grandmother looked unexpectedly sad, and DJ was curious. Did she regret missing that event all these years later?

"My mom is so excited about it," gushed Eliza. "She already booked a hotel for homecoming weekend—and she's bringing me a dress."

Grandmother brightened. "So she's coming to town then. Your father too?"

Eliza nodded happily.

"They're so sure you're going to win?" Taylor's voice was cynical. "What? Is your dad planning on buying the title for you now? Maybe he has the inside track with the vote-counting committee."

"No." Eliza narrowed her eyes at Taylor. "They just wanted to come for the fun of it. Whether I win or not. They're happy for me."

Grandmother didn't seem to notice the tension. "How nice. Perhaps your mother would like to attend the fashion show too."

"Oh, I'm sure she'd love to."

"And we'll plan a special dinner for Saturday night," continued Grandmother. "A celebration for our homecoming queen." She clapped her hands.

"How do you know we'll have a homecoming queen?" asked DJ. "After all, there's still Madison Dormont to contend with. I'm sure her family thinks that she's a shoo-in."

"*She* thinks she's a shoo-in," said Taylor.

"There's one thing we agree on," added Eliza.

"Yeah," said Kriti. "You should've heard her today. She didn't know I was behind her in the lunch line. I heard her talking to her friends, and they were all acting like the crown was hers."

"Well, her family does have some influence in this town," said Grandmother. She glanced at Eliza then Taylor. "And, as beautiful as you both are, you're newcomers to Crescent Cove."

"I don't think anyone at school cares about that," said DJ.

"Not any more than they care about silly signs and photograph buttons and chocolate," said Taylor.

"Not just chocolate," said Eliza proudly. "Godiva chocolate."

"And Starbucks coffee coupons," added Kriti.

"Oh, well, then," said Taylor with sarcasm. "That should cinch it."

"I don't know why you pick on me," said Eliza. "It's your own choice whether you campaign or not."

"Maybe I *am* campaigning," said Taylor slyly.

"In the boys' locker room," said Casey, but not quietly enough.

"Casey!" Grandmother shook her finger at her.

Casey just shrugged then excused herself. But Eliza and Kriti were suppressing giggles. To her own surprise, DJ suddenly felt defensive of Taylor.

"Well, I agree with Taylor's tactics," she said. "If it were me, I'd just let the voters decide — without the signs and buttons and chocolate."

"And coffee," added Kriti.

"Yeah. *Without* the coffee too."

Taylor reached over to give DJ a high five. And although DJ hesitated, she finally slapped palms. "Hey, you could be my campaign manager."

DJ chuckled. "And we could run the *do nothing* campaign."

"Let nature take its course," said Taylor.

"The que sera campaign."

"Whatever will be."

DJ and Taylor both laughed, but the other girls didn't look very amused. Then Grandmother tossed DJ a warning glance, although she said nothing, but DJ knew it was only because of Taylor. Grandmother didn't want to criticize her, and so she was caught in a sticky place. Finally Grandmother stood and excused herself.

"Do remember that we are a family, of sorts," she reminded them as she exited the dining room.

"A dysfunctional family," said DJ when Grandmother was out of hearing distance.

"Yes," agreed Taylor. "But we can put the fun back into dysfunctional."

Of course, DJ was well aware that she had aggravated both Eliza and Kriti by appearing to align herself with Taylor. Not that it had been her intent to do so exactly. But something about their high-profile, expensive, bribe-ish campaign was starting to seriously irritate her.

"Well, *you're* still going to help us, aren't you, Rhiannon?" asked Eliza hopefully.

Rhiannon glanced at Taylor, then turned and smiled directly at Eliza. "Sure, Eliza. I said I would and I will."

Now DJ couldn't blame Rhiannon for that. After all, Taylor had stuck it to Rhiannon enough. Why shouldn't Rhiannon support Eliza's campaign?

"And you, DJ, are not to be trusted," said Kriti.

DJ rolled her eyes. "You know what. I have decided to remain neutral on the issue of homecoming queen." She stood and reached for her crutches. "In case you haven't noticed, I have my own issues to deal with. Helping someone get elected homecoming queen just isn't very high on my priority list right now."

"Yes," said Taylor. "Let's leave the little invalid out of the fray before she gets hurt again."

"Thanks," said DJ. "From now on I shall be known as the Switzerland of homecoming."

"Our own little invalid Swiss miss," added Taylor.

DJ rolled her eyes then slowly made her way out of the dining room and up the stairs.

"How are you doing?" asked Casey as DJ shuffled across the landing toward her room.

"Tired," said DJ. "Seriously tired."

"Need any help?"

DJ considered this. Part of her wanted to take care of things herself, but she was so exhausted that it was overwhelming. "You know, Casey, I would love some help."

"At your service."

"All I want to do is get ready for bed," admitted DJ. "And I have to get everything together so that I can make it to school tomorrow."

"So you're going back?"

"Yeah. I think it's time."

"Just tell me what to do."

So, with Casey as her aid, DJ managed to get things in order and ready for bed. She thought maybe, just maybe, she would actually make it to school in the morning.

"Yeow," cried DJ as she stepped down too hard on her bad leg. She was in the bathroom trying to get into her pajama bottoms, but the boot had gotten caught up.

"You okay?" called Casey from where she'd been clearing DJ's bed and putting things away for her.

"You mean besides being in excruciating pain?"

"Want some pain medicine?"

"Yes." DJ continued to pull her pajamas on, gritting her teeth against the pain that was shooting through her leg. "I do."

"Where is it?" asked Casey as she peered into the bathroom.

DJ considered telling her, but then remembered what Taylor had said. "I'll get it," she told Casey. "Would you mind getting my wet swimsuit and towel out of the backpack in the bathroom and hanging it in the shower for me?"

Then, as Casey was doing this, DJ made her way to the sock drawer, retrieved two pills, and called to ask Casey to bring her a glass of water.

"Here you go."

DJ washed down the pills and leaned back into her pillows with a loud pain-laced groan. "Maybe somebody should just shoot me," she said. "Isn't that what they do to horses with broken legs?"

"Yeah, and they have four legs. You only have two."

"It feels like I only have one."

"Hopefully, you'll feel better after you get a good night's rest." Casey helped pull the comforter up over her. "I'd kiss you good night, but that's a little bit much for me."

"And for me," said Taylor loudly as she entered the room and peered at the two of them with a dramatically suspicious expression.

"Casey was just helping me get ready for bed." DJ let out an exasperated sigh. "And I really appreciate it."

"Speaking of helping," said Taylor. "I'd like Casey to help me too."

Casey frowned.

"Well, if you remember," said Taylor. "Not so very long ago, I decided not to press charges in a certain little scandalous affair."

"And?" Casey put her hands on her hips and looked evenly at Taylor.

"And, you told me you'd do anything—*anything*—to make up for what you did to me. Do you remember that, Casey?"

Casey nodded glumly.

"But Rhiannon took care of all that," DJ reminded her.

"Sure, she traded me her part in the musical—which by the way isn't much of a part—in exchange for excusing Casey. And I agreed to do that. But I still think Casey owes me something more."

Casey pressed her lips together and looked down. Although she wasn't saying anything, DJ felt fairly sure that Casey still felt guilty about the MySpace incident. She probably realized that, thanks to Rhiannon, she'd gotten off pretty easy.

"So what is it then?" DJ was impatient with Taylor's little cat and mouse game. Also, she was starting to feel sleepy.

"I want Casey to do something to let everyone know that she was responsible for slandering me. Whether she writes a letter to the school newspaper or takes out an ad or makes a poster or whatever, I don't care. I just want her to take full blame for the MySpace mess and make sure that everyone knows that those photos of me were tampered with by her." Taylor glared at Casey. "Is that too much to ask?"

Casey slowly shook her head. "No. I can do that."

"Is this about the homecoming queen election?" asked DJ.

"Maybe." Taylor shrugged. "Or maybe it's about my reputation."

Casey snickered.

"Go ahead and laugh," said Taylor. "But remember what they say about people in glass houses."

"Whatever." Casey went for the door now.

"But you will keep your word?" asked Taylor.

Casey narrowed her eyes and looked as if she wanted to punch someone. "If I said I will, *I will*."

"Good."

Then Casey left, firmly shutting the door behind her.

Taylor peered down at DJ. "Do you think that was too much to ask?"

"No." DJ yawned. "I actually think that was fair."

"Thank you."

"And," DJ paused dramatically, "I think you're starting to want homecoming queen more than you'll admit."

Either Taylor didn't respond, or DJ was asleep before she did.

In the morning, Taylor offered to play DJ's chauffer.

"I think someone else should ride with them," Eliza said. "My car has been pretty crowded lately."

Rhiannon didn't look interested—probably because she was still keeping a safe distance from Taylor.

"I'll go with them," Casey said reluctantly.

Casey hadn't been exactly friendly to DJ lately. And DJ had a couple of theories. 1) Casey was jealous that her volleyball skills weren't as strong as DJ's had been, or 2) Casey still resented Taylor and didn't want DJ to befriend her at all.

"Kay! See ya'll later." Eliza jingled her keys, causing Kriti and Rhiannon to grab their bags and follow her out the door, like trained pets.

"You guys ready?" asked Taylor as she checked out her hair in the foyer mirror then reapplied a thick layer of gloss over her lips.

"Don't leave without me," called Casey as DJ made her way to the front door. "I forgot something,"

"Hurry up," yelled DJ as she went out and began to maneuver down the porch steps. "We're already running late — thanks to me."

"Don't worry," said Taylor. "I'm sure they'll excuse you, and us too since you make a good reason for being late."

"Glad my handicap comes in handy for something," said DJ sarcastically.

By the time DJ got herself situated in the passenger seat, Casey was already buckling up in the backseat. Just another reminder of how slow DJ had become. She wondered if going to school this soon was a mistake.

But the morning went fairly smoothly. Sure, she was late to most of her classes and needed help carrying things, but everyone was surprisingly kind and encouraging. It was actually kind of sweet. By lunchtime she was even feeling slightly euphoric, if not sore. She'd gotten lots of pats on the back which, while physically painful, were also encouraging. Everyone seemed to think it was pretty cool that she'd risked life and limb to save Coach Jones's little boy. Still, the sooner the hoopla died down, the happier she'd be.

One benefit was that it seemed some of the prejudiced attitudes in regard to Coach Jones had also changed. Prior to the accident and the revelation of her little boy and boyfriend, a lot of kids had assumed she was gay — simply because she wore her hair short and dressed in athletic clothes and coached. To be fair, even DJ had wondered herself. Now she felt guilty about this — although she figured that Coach Jones would've forgiven her under the circumstances.

"Sit here, DJ." Eliza nudged Kriti to make room at their table, and DJ slowly eased herself down next to Eliza.

"I'll get your crutches," said Kriti, hopping up.

"And here's your lunch tray," said Casey as she set it down in front of her.

"Do you think you're going to gain some votes by having DJ sit next to you?" asked Taylor from the other end of the table.

Eliza gave her a surprised look. "I was just trying to make sure DJ was comfortable. That's all."

Of course, as DJ thought about it, she suspected that Taylor was right. Still, she wasn't about to move.

"How are you feeling?" Eliza asked DJ with what seemed like genuine concern.

"Surprisingly well." DJ stuck her straw in her soda.

"Are you on pain meds?" asked Taylor.

"Not the heavy-duty ones during school," DJ told her. "They make me too loopy. My physical therapist suggested Advil."

Talk drifted to the homecoming queen campaign. Kriti was ticked that Madison had copied them by giving away chocolates.

"But they're not Godiva," pointed out Rhiannon.

Eliza laughed. "Yes, they're just little Hershey Kisses."

"Maybe you should try giving out some real kisses," Harry teased Eliza.

"We can leave that to Taylor," said Kriti.

"As a matter of fact, Taylor has a kissing scene with Bradford today," said Eliza.

DJ glanced over to where Rhiannon was quietly eating lunch. Everyone knew this was still a sore spot for her. Although Bradford had been keeping a low profile lately, rumor was that he wanted to get back with Rhiannon. She wasn't saying much about it, and she pretended not to listen as the group bantered back and forth—stirring things up even more between Eliza and Taylor.

"I think I'm going to get a head start to drama," said DJ. "Rhiannon, would you help me with my bag?"

"I can help," offered Eliza eagerly.

"No, that's okay," said Rhiannon, quickly grabbing DJ's Hermès bag. "I've got it."

"Thanks," said DJ as Rhiannon handed her the crutches and they both started making a path for the door.

"Thank you," said Rhiannon. "That's the first time this week that I've sat with them during lunch. I should've known that someone would say something."

"So, how are you doing with that?" DJ waited for Rhiannon to push open the door to the courtyard.

Rhiannon shrugged. "I'm not sure."

"Casey said that Bradford wants to get back together with you."

"I don't know if I feel the same way."

"Yeah, that would be hard."

"I mean, I really do like him, and I've even forgiven him. But how do you forget something like that?"

"I don't know."

"So, anyway, he might as well keep his distance," said Rhiannon.

"How do you feel about his love scene with Taylor?"

Rhiannon actually laughed now. "I think I'm relieved that it's not with me. I mean, how awkward would that have been. As it is, he's been treating Taylor like a piranha."

"The boy's learning." Then DJ told Rhiannon about the deal Taylor made with Casey.

"Casey did seem a little stressed last night," admitted Rhiannon. "Despite her tough girl act, I think that girl is very tenderhearted. She just holds most of her feelings inside."

"She's always been like that."

"She needs the Lord," said Rhiannon.

"Yep."

"And, even though I hate to agree with Taylor on anything, I think it's only fair that Casey does straighten that whole thing out with her."

"I know. I wouldn't tell Casey this, but I do think she got off a little too easily. Taylor could've taken her to court."

At the end of the day, DJ wasn't feeling quite as on top of things as she had earlier. The fun and newness slowly wore off and now she felt mostly tired and sore. Still, she had promised Conner that she'd go to his soccer match.

"Are you sure you don't want to go home now?" asked Taylor as she jingled DJ's car keys in front of her.

"I do want to go home," admitted DJ. "But I told Conner I'd watch his game."

"How about if we just watch half of it?" suggested Taylor.

DJ wanted to ask about the "we" part, since she hadn't exactly invited Taylor to join her, but maybe Taylor was just trying to be helpful.

"Okay," agreed DJ. "Unless it's a really good game or I get my second wind. In that case, I might want to stay for the whole thing."

"Sure," said Taylor. "Whatever."

But as soon as they got to the game, DJ didn't know if she wanted to stay at all.

"What's wrong?" asked Taylor when DJ stopped part way through the stands. "Is your leg hurting?"

DJ shook her head and just stared down at the field where Conner and Haley were standing and talking. Okay, that shouldn't have been a big deal, but something about the way Conner was looking at Haley, something about the distance between them—like two inches—well, it made DJ's stomach twist into a tight knot.

"Oh." Taylor nodded. "I think I see the problem."

"It's probably nothing." But DJ just kept standing there, unsure whether to continue on or not.

"Do you want to leave?"

DJ pressed her lips together as she continued watching Conner talking to Haley. He was totally oblivious to her. And why wouldn't he be? There before him was a beautiful little pixie girl, her head tilted up, her eyes all sparkling. She adored him. And he was eating it up!

"We can just turn and leave, DJ," said Taylor quietly.

"Okay." Of course, that was easier said than done. Pivoting herself in the narrow walkway between bleachers required careful coordination, but finally DJ was turned around and going as quickly as her crutches would carry her away from there. She didn't pause until they were safely hidden in the stairway that led into the stadium.

Taylor didn't say anything as they continued out and toward the parking lot. All DJ could think was, why not? Why wouldn't Conner prefer Haley to her? Besides the fact that Haley was pretty and nice and smart—wasn't that how Conner had first described her to DJ—she was ambulatory!

"I'm sorry," said Taylor once they were in the car.

DJ turned and looked at her with surprise. "Oh. Yeah. Thanks."

"If that was what it looked like, I think Conner is an idiot and a jerk."

"Maybe." DJ felt tears burning now, but she was determined not to cry. At least not here. Not now. "But to be fair, I'm not a lot of fun these days. And Conner is an active guy. He likes sports. He needs a girlfriend who can keep up."

Taylor said a foul word.

"Anyway," DJ tried to sound more positive. "It might be nothing."

"If it was nothing, why did we leave?"

"Because I really am tired," said DJ. "Going to the soccer match was probably a dumb idea."

"Works for me." Taylor started the car and pulled out a little quickly from the parking lot.

"Hey," yelled DJ. "Take it easy, will ya?"

Taylor slowed down now. "Sorry. I guess I tend to be an emotional driver."

"Then you should be careful on your Vespa," warned DJ as she turned on her CD player. She was trying not to think about Conner and Haley.

"Hey, turn that one up," said Taylor.

So DJ cranked it up and Taylor started singing along. To her own surprise, DJ did too. And they actually sounded pretty good together. Well, as long as the volume was up. But it did help DJ to forget, at least for now.

Once they were home, Taylor sat down on the porch and shook out a cigarette. "Care to join me?" she asked DJ.

DJ made a face. "Yeah, right." Then she looked around and realized that it was really a nice day — one of those last days in September when it felt almost like summer. Sitting on the sunny porch sounded kind of tempting. "I'd join you," she told Taylor, "not for a cigarette, but just for the sunshine. But I need to take a pain pill."

"Want me to get one for you?" asked Taylor.

DJ considered this. It was actually very tempting. But, on the other hand, she didn't really want Taylor to know she'd hidden them. "That's okay," she said slowly. "I need to use the bathroom anyway."

"Want something cool to drink?" Taylor took a slow drag.

"Yeah, that'd be nice."

"Okay, let me finish this up, and I'll go get us something."

DJ knew that Taylor was being nice to her because she felt sorry about the deal with Conner. Still, DJ appreciated it. She used the bathroom and went for her sock drawer, but when she opened up the sock, she noticed that—once again—there seemed to be pills missing. She shook them out into her hand to see that there were eight pills. That meant about ten had been taken! Someone had found her secret stash. She took two with water and put the remaining six pills in a Kleenex and stuck them in her jeans pocket. She went back downstairs where Taylor was already setting out a couple of sodas as well as a small bowl of pretzels on the table.

"Taylor," said DJ in a firm voice. "Do you happen to know where I put my Vicodin?"

"Huh?" Taylor looked up.

"My Vicodin pills—have you seen them?"

"Not since you were staying in Inez's room downstairs. Why? Did someone take them again?" Taylor shook out another cigarette.

DJ just stared at Taylor, trying to determine if she was telling the truth or not. She certainly looked unconcerned enough. But she was also a good actress.

"I thought you were going to hide them really well this time," said Taylor as she popped open a can.

"I did."

"Apparently not. Where did you hide them anyway?"

DJ sat down and folded her arms across her chest.

"Look," Taylor said, "it doesn't matter if you tell me since that spot obviously didn't work."

"In my sock drawer."

Taylor laughed. "In your sock drawer? That's almost as bad as in your underwear drawer."

"What do you mean?"

"That's where people always go looking for valuable things, DJ. It's always the underwear drawer first — you know, way in the back behind a lacy bra. Then the sock drawer. Then the jewelry box. Then under the mattress. The obvious places."

"Oh." DJ reached for a soda and frowned. "I guess that makes sense."

"Did she take all of them?"

"No, I have eight left."

Taylor shook her head. "So, what are you going to do? I'm sure your doctor is going to wonder why you're using so much Vicodin."

"Fortunately, I think I can get by just using it at bedtime."

"So that gives you four nights?"

"Actually three. I just took two."

"Oh." Taylor scowled. "Well, that just sucks, DJ. Someone in the house is taking your pills, and you're the one who will suffer."

"I know."

"I know you don't want me to say this, but I bet it's Casey."

"Why?"

"Because of a conversation I had with her when she first moved here."

"What did she say?"

"She admitted that she'd had a little substance abuse problem before."

"Really?" DJ considered this. "She didn't tell me."

"I don't think she was exactly proud of it." Taylor blew out a puff of smoke. "But she caught me smoking and I think that made her feel like she could trust me." Taylor laughed now. "Not that she does anymore."

Somehow this made sense. Casey had told DJ a few things, and she'd also left out a few things. Still, DJ hated to think …

"Casey was in your room last night," pointed out Taylor. "Helping you get ready for bed."

"Yes, but she was in the bathroom when I took my pills."

"Did she know you were taking your pills?"

DJ tried to remember. "Well, yeah, because she was getting me a glass of water. But she wasn't in the room when I got them."

"Think about it," said Taylor. "All she'd need to do is peek through the crack in the bathroom door. She could plainly see the bedside table from there."

DJ looked suspiciously at Taylor now. "How would you know?"

"It's geometry. Think about it."

"Maybe."

"Oh, and remember when Casey suddenly needed to get something upstairs when we were all heading to school this morning. What was up with that?"

DJ took a sip of soda and considered this. "I suppose it's possible."

"She had motive and opportunity."

DJ rolled her eyes. "What are you, Nancy Drew?"

Taylor laughed.

"So what should I do about it?" asked DJ.

"Confront her."

"You mean accuse her?"

"Accuse, confront, whatever trips your trigger." Taylor picked up a pretzel. "As I recall, you accused me, didn't you?"

DJ sighed. "Yeah, but you make it so easy. Everyone wants to accuse you of everything."

"So I've noticed."

"I think you enjoy being the bad girl, Taylor. It's like an addiction, or you need the attention or something."

"Or maybe it's just easier than being good."

"I CAN'T BELIEVE YOU," said Casey hotly.

DJ took in a slow breath. "I'm just asking."

"If I took your Vicodin?"

"That's what I said." DJ watched Casey's expression go from angry to hurt and back to angry again.

"I thought you were my friend."

"I am your friend, Casey. But I think you might have a problem."

"Me?" Her voice was getting pretty loud now. DJ got worried that the other girls might overhear them. She'd asked Casey to meet her in the library and then even closed the door. For Casey's sake, she wanted to keep this private.

DJ just nodded. "Can't we just talk in a civilized manner?"

"Why would I want to talk to you?" Casey stood and went to the door.

"If you have a problem—"

"You're the one with the problem," said Casey. "To go around accusing your friends of stealing your drugs. Sheesh!"

"I just asked you, and—"

"Asked, accused—what's the difference?" Casey turned and looked at DJ with a wounded expression. "And why me anyway? Why wouldn't you have accused someone else? For instance, Taylor? Now that at least makes sense. Or how about the housekeeper or the cook? Or even your grandmother—we all know she's a little loopy sometimes."

DJ watched as Casey reached for the doorknob, as if getting ready to leave. "If it makes you feel better, I did accuse Taylor."

"And, naturally, she denied it."

"Quite believably too."

"Meaning you *don't* believe me?" Casey glared at DJ now.

DJ didn't want to admit it, but she was a little stunned by Casey's angry reaction. She had tried to do this very gently, just mentioning that some pills were gone, and suddenly Casey had gone ballistic.

"Well, think what you want to, DJ. I think this whole hero business has gone straight to your head. Or maybe you've been overdosing on your stupid pills. But you are flipping nuts!" Casey stormed out, slamming the door behind her.

"What's going on between you and Casey?" Rhiannon asked DJ as the two of them met at the foot of the stairs.

"Nothing," muttered DJ. She wished she hadn't mentioned this to anyone. What a mess.

"Well, it looked like more than nothing to me. She was enraged, and she told me you'd lost your mind."

"I just asked her about something, and she got offended."

"Anything serious?"

DJ shrugged.

"Anything I can help you with?"

DJ knew she could trust Rhiannon. She also knew that she needed some help—and some perspective. It was one thing to listen to Taylor, but Taylor didn't always show the best judgment, or morals. DJ tipped her head toward the library, and Rhiannon led the way. DJ followed her in, gently closing the door behind her. "You can't tell anyone, okay?"

Rhiannon nodded. "What's up?"

So DJ quietly retold the story from the beginning, and Rhiannon thoughtfully listened.

"So you really don't think it's Taylor then?"

"I really don't. I mean, I realize that Taylor would be the usual suspect and that she's been known to lie, but I think I can sort of read her. And, I'm almost beginning to understand her a little."

Rhiannon frowned like she wasn't so sure. "And what makes you so certain that it's really Casey?"

"I'm not, actually," DJ said. "But her reaction makes me wonder. It was so abrupt. I mean, she wasn't even rational. She wouldn't even discuss it with me. And when Taylor told me about Casey's confession, well, it sort of rang true to me."

Rhiannon nodded like she agreed. "I promised I wouldn't tell anyone this, DJ. But under the circumstances, I think I should."

DJ waited.

"Casey told me that she'd had an addiction problem, and that was one of the reasons her parents decided to send her here. They thought her friends had been a bad influence, and I'd have to agree, since that's when she started experimenting with drugs."

"What kinds of drugs?"

"Mostly prescription. Her friends were good at stealing them. And Casey's mom had an old prescription for oxycontin."

"Isn't that supposed to be really bad?"

"To be honest, I don't know. I mean, my mom's obviously got her own favorite drug of choice — nothing seems quite as bad as that. I suppose I was sort of trying to forget about what Casey had told me, hoping that it was something she'd left back in California." Rhiannon looked like she was about to cry now. "It's like I can't get away from this."

"I'm so sorry, Rhiannon," said DJ suddenly. "I totally forgot about your mom's situation. How's she doing anyway?"

"They're saying she needs a year of treatment. Heroine is pretty nasty stuff, DJ."

"I know."

Rhiannon sniffed. "And she actually seems in good spirits — much better than when she first went in."

"I need to remember to pray for her more."

"Thanks."

DJ shook her head. "I can't believe that Casey told you and Taylor . . . then left me totally in the dark."

"The reason she told me was because I told her about my mom."

"Oh."

"She thought I'd understand. Plus, I think she thought it would make me feel better."

"And she knew she could trust you."

"But now I've told you."

The girls stared at each other for a moment. "If I tell Grandmother, Casey will be out of here," DJ said. "I know it."

Rhiannon nodded. "And it seemed like she'd sort of turned a corner. I mean, she's even been letting me talk to her about God and everything."

"So what do we do?"

Rhiannon's eyes lit up. "Another intervention."

DJ remembered their fashion intervention with Casey and how well that had worked. Sure, they'd taken Casey by surprise, and she'd gotten pretty mad to start with, but with all the girls explaining why she needed to change her appearance (mostly to keep Grandmother from kicking her out) Casey had eventually given in.

"You know," DJ said slowly, "that's not a bad idea. We could confront her and tell her that we've talked and that we know what she's doing."

"And that we want to help her," added Rhiannon.

"The question is whether to include everyone or not." DJ frowned. "Drugs are a lot more serious than fashion."

"And Kriti would probably freak if she heard that someone in this house is taking drugs," said Rhiannon. "She has a serious phobia about drugs. She told me."

"Well, the only girls who don't know about this are Eliza and Kriti."

"And they went to Harry's house," said Rhiannon. "To work on something for the campaign, something they didn't want Taylor to know about."

"Like she cares."

"How about if we do the intervention tonight?"

"I don't know." Suddenly DJ had cold feet. "Casey was so mad already. What if she does something crazy—goes into a rage, or runs away, or something?"

"My guess is that if she stole your Vicodin and if she is as mad as it seemed just now, then she's probably already taken a pill or two by now. She'll probably be totally chill." Rhiannon's brow creased. "In fact, come to think of it, she's been pretty chill a couple of times when I would've thought she'd have been losing it."

"Like after they lost the match?" said DJ.

"Yeah. Remember how she was so laid back that night?"

"So how do we do this? When and where do we do the intervention?" asked DJ.

"My guess is that she's in our room now. How about we do it there? And there's no time like now."

"Okay. Should we talk to Taylor first?"

Rhiannon frowned.

"You don't think Taylor should be involved?"

"Uh," Rhiannon said. She looked about to say no, but then she shrugged. "She should probably be involved. Especially if Casey already told her about her problem."

"But you don't want her there?" asked DJ.

"It's just me." Rhiannon shrugged. "But maybe we need Taylor. At least she's good at getting to the point."

"So do we need some kind of plan?"

"Probably." Rhiannon stood. "Let's go talk to Taylor. She might have some ideas."

"An intervention?" Taylor set aside the fashion magazine that she'd been perusing, exhaling loudly as if exasperated.

"You don't have to participate if you don't want to," said DJ. "We just thought that because Casey had confided in—"

"No, it's okay." Taylor reached for her bag, removing a small black notebook and a sleek silver pen. "It's just that interventions aren't exactly fun. But if we're going to do it, we should at least be prepared."

DJ felt surprised, but relieved. "Yeah, that's kind of what we thought too."

"What are our demands?" asked Taylor.

"Demands?" echoed DJ.

"Like our expectations," suggested Rhiannon.

"You say to-mah-to and I say to-may-to," said Taylor. "What are we asking Casey to commit to here? Does she need rehab? Does she need counseling? What?"

"It's kind of hard to say without knowing the extent of her problem, don't you think?" said Rhiannon.

Taylor almost smiled. "Good point. For starters we'll ask her to tell us the truth about what and how much she's using."

"What if she refuses to cooperate?" asked DJ.

"Then we hold her feet to the fire," said Taylor with an evil glint in her eye.

"Huh?" DJ stared at her.

"What kind of fire?" asked Rhiannon without batting an eyelash.

"See," said Taylor, nodding to Rhiannon. "She gets this."

DJ just shrugged. "Fine. What kind of fire?"

"Something she doesn't want—like being sent home," said Rhiannon.

"Exactly," said Taylor.

"And if we told my grandmother, she would most definitely be sent home."

"That's true," said Taylor. "It almost happened already."

"Twice," pointed out DJ.

"Yes," said Rhiannon. "This could be the third strike."

"Okay," continued Taylor. "We make her tell us the truth—then what?"

"Like Rhiannon said, won't it depend on how messed up she is?"

"Yes. But we need a plan."

"We need to make her promise to get help," said Rhiannon. "I know a good drug counselor in town. That would be a place to start."

"Sounds like we have a plan." Taylor stood now. "You girls ready?"

"I want to pray first," said Rhiannon.

Taylor just shrugged and waited.

"Dear Heavenly Father," prayed Rhiannon, "we really do love Casey and we want the best for her. Please help her to see that we're confronting her in love. Please soften her heart to hear us. And help us to find the answers that you think are best. Amen."

"Amen," echoed DJ.

"Let's go," said Taylor.

"I can't believe you guys are ganging up on me like this," complained Casey. She was sitting on her bed now, backed up against the headboard with her knees pulled up to her chin. DJ thought she looked something like a trapped animal. Maybe that's how she felt.

"We're not ganging up on you," said Rhiannon calmly. "We're trying to help you."

"But we need you to be honest." DJ held up the empty prescription bottle as if it were evidence.

"And seriously," said Taylor, "there are worse things in the world than abusing prescription drugs."

Casey narrowed her eyes at Taylor. "Yeah, and you've probably done most of them."

Taylor just smiled. "Maybe so, Casey. So why not fess up. Join the bad-girl club. Seems to me you were a member not that long ago."

Casey closed her eyes tightly and pulled her knees even closer to her chin. "Just go away!" she seethed. "Leave me alone."

DJ glanced at the others. Taylor just shrugged and looked like maybe she was actually going to leave. And Rhiannon looked like she was on the verge of tears. Maybe this was hitting too close to home for her . . . maybe she was remembering her mother.

"Look, Case," said DJ gently. She moved over and sat on the bed near Casey now. "We really do want to help you. And you know I can't let this go. Even my physical therapist said so."

"You told her about me?" Casey looked alarmed.

"No, not specifically. I just told her my pills had been disappearing."

"And why is that my problem?" asked Casey with angry eyes. "Why am I the one you decided to accuse?" She glanced over to where Taylor was comfortably seated in an armchair, one leg crossed over the other and simply observing this scene as if she were watching a rerun of *The OC*. "Why not her?"

"Because I have a gut feeling about this, Casey." DJ bit her lip and shot up a silent prayer for help. "And I really need you to be honest right now."

Casey said nothing . . . just shut her eyes again, pressing her lips tightly together.

"Look, Casey," said DJ more firmly. "I can't pretend like nothing's wrong here."

"Nothing is wrong," Casey said quietly. "Just give it a rest, okay . . ."

"I really care about you, Casey. I can't just give it a rest."

Now Rhiannon joined them on the bed, sitting on the other side of Casey. "Honest, Casey, we just really care about you. You know that, don't you?"

Casey shrugged.

DJ reached over and put her hand on Casey's arm. "Casey, we've been friends for . . . well, for almost forever. And I've never intentionally hurt you, have I?"

Casey shook her head then looked back down at her knees.

"And I thought I was your friend too," added Rhiannon.

"You are," muttered Casey. "You both are. But I don't see why you can't let this go."

"Because we love you, Casey," said DJ. "We don't want to lose you."

"Why would you lose me?"

"Because Mrs. Carter will kick you out," said Taylor.

DJ tossed a warning glance at Taylor, but Taylor just shrugged. "It's the truth and you know it."

"Why does she have to know?" demanded Casey.

"So are you admitting you took the Vicodin?" asked DJ.

Casey sort of nodded, but didn't say a word.

"And the first step to recovery is admitting you've got a problem," said Rhiannon quietly.

"Fine," snapped Casey. "I have a problem. Are you guys happy now?"

"I'm glad you're being honest," said DJ. "I'm not happy you have a problem."

"But maybe we can help you," said Rhiannon.

"How?" demanded Casey. Her expression was angry, but DJ thought she could see tears in her eyes.

"There are lots of ways to get help," said Rhiannon. "But for starters you need to be completely truthful with us."

"Okay," said Casey slowly. She looked directly at DJ now. "I did take your Vicodin, DJ." She took in a deep breath. "Both times."

"Why?" asked DJ.

"I don't know."

"Had you been using all along?" asked Taylor.

"No." Casey firmly shook her head. "Honestly, I haven't. But I saw that bottle sitting by DJ's bed. I picked it up and shook it. I just wanted to shake it."

"Why?" asked DJ again. She so did not get this.

"I don't know ... but the sound of those pills ..." Casey sighed. "I think I was feeling stressed ... and the pills seemed like an answer."

"That makes sense," said Taylor. She had moved to the foot of Casey's bed now, and she actually had a thoughtful look on her face. "I know how that feels."

Casey nodded slowly. "So while DJ was in the bathroom, I snuck a pill. Just one pill."

"And?" persisted Rhiannon. "Tell the whole story, Casey."

"And it felt good." Casey sort of smiled. "Okay, it felt really good. It was like this load was lifted, and I felt all relaxed and good."

"It's not like that when I take them," said DJ. "I just get sleepy."

"Everyone's different," said Rhiannon.

"So you took one," said Taylor. "And one led to another . . . and another."

Casey nodded. "Yeah."

"But how did you find them in my sock drawer?" asked DJ.

"I watched you get them." Casey shrugged. "It was easy."

"Well, you won't find them again."

"Do you have any left?" Rhiannon asked Casey.

Casey didn't answer.

"Tell us, Casey," said Taylor. "Do you have any left?"

Casey swallowed hard and looked back down at her knees again.

"Where are they?" asked Taylor. "Tell us before we have to look for—"

"In my bag," said Casey quickly.

Taylor went for Casey's black leather purse. "Do you want to tell me where or should I just dump it?"

Casey said nothing.

"Come on, Casey," said Rhiannon. "You know that DJ needs those pills. Think about it, okay. She's in pain, and you took the pills that help her not to be in pain. Doesn't that mean anything to you?"

Casey had even more tears in her eyes as she looked up at DJ. "Yeah. It does. I'm sorry, DJ. Hand me the purse, Taylor, you'll never find them."

Taylor chuckled. "Don't be too sure." But she handed the bag over.

As it turned out, Taylor probably wouldn't have found them. DJ was fairly certain that she never would've herself. Casey had a secret pocket that she'd put into the bottom of her purse. She fished a Ziploc bag out and poured the pills into DJ's hand. There were only five pills left, but it was better than nothing.

"When did you last take one?" asked Taylor.

"About thirty minutes ago."

"After our fight?" asked DJ.

Casey just nodded.

Now DJ slipped her arm around Casey and gave her a sideways squeeze. "You know that drugs are not the real answer, don't you?"

Casey didn't say anything.

"Drugs are a bogus solution that just drags you deeper and deeper into trouble until you can't get out," added Rhiannon. "I've seen it close up. I know how destructive—how deceptive—drugs can be."

"Rhiannon and I don't agree on much," said Taylor, "but she's right on about that. I've seen it too."

"So will you go see the counselor I told you about?" asked Rhiannon. "She's really nice. She helped my mom find help."

Casey looked scared now. "What about my parents? Will the counselor tell them?"

"I don't know." Rhiannon glanced at the others. "I mean, I know there's that doctor-patient confidentiality thing, but I'm not sure what happens when you're a minor."

"I don't know either," admitted DJ.

"I'll go with you," offered Rhiannon.

"So ... you'll go then, Casey?" asked DJ. "You'll get some help?"

"Your only other option is for us to tell Mrs. Carter," Taylor said firmly. "You know we will. At least I will. And then you'll be sent home for certain."

"And then your parents will know for certain," said DJ.

"I think it would be good for them to know anyway," declared Rhiannon. Then Casey gave her a worried look. "I mean eventually," added Rhiannon. "You know, when the time is right."

Casey wiped her wet cheeks and looked at the three girls huddled around her. "I guess I don't have much choice, do I?"

"No, not really," stated Taylor.

Now Casey actually smiled. "With friends like you guys, who needs—"

"Drugs?" offered Taylor with a sly grin. "You're absolutely right."

DJ was surprised when Casey actually laughed at this. In fact, it seemed like Casey was relieved. Sad and embarrassed for sure, but also relieved.

DJ HAD TURNED OFF HER CELL phone after she'd gotten home that afternoon. She knew that it was possible that Conner might try to call her after the soccer game ended. She also knew it was possible that he might not. She just wasn't sure which she would prefer, and keeping her phone turned off kept it simple. Still, once she was in bed waiting for her pain pill to kick in and remove the throbbing, she wondered if he had tried to call. She wondered if he even missed her at the game.

The next morning, as she got ready for school, she decided her best course of action would be to pretend like nothing had happened. Unless Conner brought it up, she would not. She would keep a friendly but cool distance. It would be up to him to straighten things out.

"So what do you think is going to happen with Conner?" Taylor asked as she drove DJ and Casey to school.

DJ glanced in the backseat to see if Casey was listening. She'd been so quiet this morning that DJ thought she was consumed with thoughts of what would come out of last night's intervention.

"What's going on with Conner?" asked Casey with mild interest.

"You didn't tell her?" said Taylor.

"I never really had a chance." DJ shrugged. "Besides, I don't really know anyway. There's not much to tell."

"Come on," urged Casey. "Tell me. Maybe it'll take my mind off my own stupid problems."

"Can I tell her?" asked Taylor.

"Whatever." Then DJ listened as Taylor gave an account of Conner and Haley at the soccer game yesterday, making it sound even worse than DJ had thought it was.

"Oh, I'm sorry, DJ." Casey's voice was actually pretty sympathetic.

"Well, we might've been reading more into it," said DJ defensively. "I mean they're old friends. She was probably just telling him to have a good game and stuff like that."

"Yeah, right," said Taylor with skepticism. "It looked to me like they were planning their elopement and how many children they planned to have."

"Thanks." DJ sighed loudly.

"That just bites," said Casey. "Like it's not bad enough that you've got a broken leg and your friend steals your pain pills, but then your boyfriend goes and breaks up with—"

"He didn't break up." But even as DJ said this, she knew it was probably inevitable. "Yet."

"Maybe you should break up first," said Taylor.

"Yeah," said Casey. "That might take some of the sting out."

DJ knew that breaking up with Conner might protect her pride some, but she really did like Conner. What if her assumptions about how Conner felt about Haley were wrong? What if Haley was simply flirting with him, and he was just trying to be nice about it? What if Conner still really liked

DJ? How would he feel if she dumped him for all the wrong reasons? "I don't know," she finally said as they pulled into the school parking lot.

"Well, think about it," said Taylor. "If you see him coming at you with it, just slap him with your news first. Tell him he's history."

"That's right," said Casey. "Let him have it."

DJ felt pretty sure that she wasn't going to "let him have it," but she nodded to humor them. And throughout the morning, she kept a lookout for him. But it wasn't until lunchtime that she saw him.

"Hey, stranger," Conner said as he joined her by the cafeteria entrance.

"Hey," she said back.

"How's the leg?"

She shrugged. "Kind of sore."

"Is that why you skipped out of the game yesterday?"

"Um, yeah."

"Haley said she met you at the pool. She said she really likes you and that she offered to give you rides to the pool after school."

DJ didn't feel like talking about Haley. "Well, I didn't go yesterday. I thought I was going to your match."

He nodded. "Yeah, Haley had gone that early morning anyway, but you could probably get a ride with her this afternoon, if you want."

"Sounds like you and Haley have been spending a lot of time together," DJ said, watching closely for his reaction. So far his conversation about Haley had seemed rather casual and innocent. But now his neck reddened slightly.

"Yeah. I think she's kind of lonely."

"But doesn't she know lots of people here? I mean, since she used to live here all those years."

"You'd think so. But some of her old friends, like Madison Dormont and Tina Clark, have gotten kind of snooty."

DJ couldn't help but make a face. "She was friends with Madison and Tina?"

"In middle school. Trust me, both of them were nicer back then. Anyway, I was telling her about you, DJ. I think you guys could be friends."

"Well, I'll ask her for a ride to the pool this afternoon," said DJ. But as soon as she said this, she regretted it. She really didn't want to spend time with Conner's old girlfriend. If she was really his "old" girlfriend. DJ still wasn't convinced that something new wasn't brewing.

"That's great," said Conner, seeming genuinely excited. "Why don't you tell me what you want for lunch, and I'll pick it up while you go sit down?"

So she told him and then she smiled and thought, really, Conner was such a sweet guy and he really did care about her—why should she doubt him? Then as she made her way toward where her friends were already gathering at their regular table, she noticed Haley standing by herself near the girls' restroom. Haley smiled and waved, but DJ was surprised to see how nervous she looked. Haley was like the golden girl, and she was nervous?

DJ paused. "Hey, Haley," she called out. "Do you want to eat lunch at our table?"

Haley's eyes lit up, and she nodded eagerly. "Sure, thanks."

"I'll save you a place," said DJ with a smile that felt as genuine as a three dollar bill. She really didn't want to share her Conner-time with Haley, but neither could she stand to leave a lonely girl lonely.

168

DJ saved a spot for Haley on one side of her and another for Conner on the other side. As soon as Haley walked up with a lunch tray, DJ introduced her to her friends, although it seemed everyone had already met her.

"It's hard being the new girl back in your own home town," admitted Haley. "Thanks for letting me sit with you guys."

Just then Conner joined them. He looked slightly taken aback to see Haley sitting next to DJ, but he smiled at both of them then took his seat next to DJ. "Did you tell Haley that you want to bum a ride to the pool this afternoon?" asked Conner.

Haley, overhearing this, leaned over and grinned at them. "No problem."

"That means I'm off the hook for chauffeuring?" asked Taylor.

"Totally," said Haley. "I can bring DJ home too."

"It's so fun being the poor handicapped girl," joked DJ. "Everyone has to take care of you and be nice to you."

"At least until the big election," teased Taylor. "Then some people—" she elbowed Eliza now, "will probably go back to being mean again."

"I've never been mean to DJ," said Eliza.

"Don't get all defensive," said Taylor. "I'm just kidding."

"It must be interesting having two candidates for home-coming queen under the same roof," observed Haley.

"Interesting is one word for it," said DJ.

"I can think of some four-letter words that come to mind when I think about it," said Taylor.

"And she uses them too," said Eliza in a prissy sort of voice.

"I used to dream of being homecoming queen too ..." Haley sighed sadly.

"Hey, you could be a write-in," suggested Conner. "That happened one year when my sister was running."

"A write-in?" She laughed. "Who would possibly write me in?"

The table got uncomfortably quiet now.

"Okay," said DJ quickly. "Let me warn you, Haley. That's a dangerous question in this crowd. We already have people scrapping for votes here. I had to declare myself neutral . . . as in Switzerland."

"Yes we call her the Swiss Miss," said Rhiannon.

Everyone laughed.

"Well, I wouldn't even know how to launch a write-in campaign anyway," admitted Haley.

"Oh, it's probably not much different than what people are doing now," said Conner.

"Some people aren't doing anything," said Taylor proudly.

"Taylor is running a non-campaign," explained DJ. "No signs, no gimmicks. She's kind of a stealth candidate."

"Don't be so sure about that," said Casey. Then Garrison winked at her like they were in cahoots about something. DJ wanted to ask, but the bell rang and everyone took off in different directions.

By the end of the day, DJ knew what Casey had been up to. In fact, the whole school knew—thanks to the school radio station, WCCS, which was available in the classrooms. As it turned out, Casey had put the station to good use to keep her promise to Taylor. This made perfect sense since the station manager was none other than Garrison McKinley. Anyway, he must've allowed her to record a public announcement, and it was played several times throughout the afternoon. DJ heard it twice. She had to give Casey points for cleverness when she listened to the little poem that exonerated Taylor, defending

170

her reputation, and giving Casey full credit for posting the skanky photos on the Internet. DJ was sure that Taylor would be pleased.

"What was that thing on the radio about?" asked Haley as she drove them to the pool. So DJ explained what Casey had done to get even with Taylor for hurting Rhiannon. It actually came in handy since it filled in the dead space and prevented DJ from demanding to know what Haley's intentions toward Conner were. Also, DJ couldn't miss the irony of how the reason Taylor got slandered was because she'd moved in on Rhiannon's boyfriend. She wondered if Haley had picked up on that.

"Man, you girls must have some wild times at Carter House," said Haley as they went up the steps the led to the pool building. "Kind of like being in a sorority."

"Oh, yeah, it's the blast that lasts." DJ made her way into the dressing room, careful to avoid a puddle that looked slick.

"Do you need any help?" offered Haley.

"No, that's okay. I know you need to practice, and it'll probably take me a few minutes to get ready. You go ahead." DJ was actually relieved to go into the cubicle and sit down on the metal bench. The process of dressing and undressing was still a painful challenge, and she was already tired from a full day at school. But at least she'd come up with a good solution for the pool this morning. She had decided to wear her bikini like underwear. That way she could simply take off her jeans and T-shirt and be ready to go.

Of course, she hadn't considered the reaction she would get as she crutched her way out to the deck. A couple of the swim team guys actually whistled. Well, fine, she thought. She could deal with that. She paused, and balancing herself on her crutches, she feigned blowing a kiss, mouthing the words "thank you" as if addressing adoring fans. Naturally, this just made them whistle more. She rolled her eyes then proceeded toward the lane that was vacant.

"Hey, DJ," said Caleb as he descended from the lifeguard chair. "How's it going?"

She smiled. "Slightly better than the last time I was here." She handed him her crutches and held onto the pool ladder. "Hopefully I remember how to do this."

"Looks like the bruising is fading."

She glanced at her leg and nodded. "Yeah. It is looking a little better. Still kind of Frankenstein-ish though. Too bad Halloween's a month away. I could've taken my leg out trick-or-treating."

He laughed as she eased herself into the water.

"There," she said once she was fully in. "Was that better than last time?"

He nodded. "Much better."

"Wish it felt better," she said as she attempted a small kick.

"No pain, no gain." He grinned.

And normally she would've agreed with that old sports slogan. But the kind of pain she'd experienced since the accident hadn't seemed to have gained her much of anything. And the sooner it ended, the happier she would be. But she faithfully, albeit slowly, swam laps for an hour. And then, once again, as she painfully extracted herself from the water, Caleb stuck out his arm to help her.

"Thanks," she said, struggling to get her crutches into place and wishing she'd brought a towel.

"You were moving faster today," he said.

"I used to be able to swim fairly well," she said sadly.

"You will again."

"I hope so."

"Give yourself time."

She nodded. "Yeah, I know." And she knew enough about sports to grasp that it took hard work to get better at anything. Unfortunately, when it came to athletics, she'd never had to work so hard for so little in her life.

He patted her on the back. "Have a good weekend, DJ."

"Thanks. You too." Then she hobbled back to the dressing room. And this time when she took a shower, she soaped up and shampooed her hair, but the bikini remained intact until she was in the dressing room and behind the curtain in the cubicle. No more strippers on crutches scenes for this girl!

Back in Haley's car, DJ tried desperately to keep from mentioning Conner, which was all she could think about. She complimented Haley on her car, a classic VW Bug. "Where do you get something like this?"

"My dad got it on eBay and then restored it for me," she explained. "It's almost forty years old."

"Cool. I'll bet it gets good gas mileage too."

"Unfortunately, the older models don't do as well as the new ones."

DJ didn't know much about cars, so the conversation went nowhere. They fell quiet again.

"DJ?" ventured Haley. "Are you and Conner fairly serious? I mean, I know you date sometimes, but are you like a serious couple?"

DJ shrugged. "I guess it depends on how you define serious."

"Well, like exclusive."

"We've never said we were exclusive, but I guess I sort of assumed that we were." DJ considered telling Haley about how she and Conner had dated briefly during the summer, followed by a breakup that had nearly broken her heart, but decided not to. Why let Haley know that DJ sometimes felt insecure in her relationship with Conner?

"Yeah. Okay." Haley bit her lip. "Sorry, I shouldn't have asked."

"That's all right." DJ knew she should change the subject now, but something inside wouldn't let her. "Do you still like him?"

Haley didn't answer. And DJ knew that was her answer.

"Does he still like you?" DJ asked in a small voice.

Again Haley didn't say anything, and the silence in the car was so thick that it felt like it was cutting off the oxygen supply. DJ had the urge to open the window.

"I'd like to lie to you, DJ," said Haley finally. "I'd like to say, no, I have absolutely no interest in Conner. But the truth is I still have feelings for him. Still, I respect that you guys are a couple."

"Do you think Conner has feelings for you?" asked DJ weakly.

Haley just shrugged. "It's not like he's said anything."

"But you think he does?"

"I don't know." Haley sighed. "You know how guys can be."

DJ wanted to say that, no, Conner wasn't like that. Unlike other guys, Conner was actually pretty good at sharing his feelings, and that was one of the reasons she liked him so much. She wanted to say that they had this special connection, that they'd made it through that one miserable misunderstanding last summer, and she hoped that meant they could make it through another, although she wasn't positive. She thought that things were cool between her and Conner now. But she didn't say anything.

And when Haley dropped her off at Carter House, she barely even said good-bye.

"I WISH IT WASN'T AN AWAY GAME," DJ told Conner on the phone. She was lying on her bed with her legs propped up on a pillow and her eyes closed. She had just managed to settle in when he called, and it had taken every ounce of energy she had to reach over and pick up her cell phone. She had been glad to hear from him, but when he'd invited her to a football game, she'd groaned. It was an hour's drive, which meant they would get home late—plus she had to get up early to go to an appointment with the physical therapist the next day. "I'm not sure that I'm up for that," she said. What she was hoping was that he'd think of something else for them to do—maybe get a bite to eat at the Hammerhead. Fish and chips sounded good to her.

"I'd really like to see that game," he said wistfully. "But I understand that you're tired, DJ. You're making an amazing comeback. It's hard to believe it was a week ago that you jumped in front of that Suburban."

It wasn't hard for her to believe it. Her leg was throbbing like crazy, and she'd already taken several Advil pills. "Why don't you go ahead and go to the game without me. I think Harry and Eliza are going. You could tag along with them."

He laughed. "Eliza never talks about anything besides homecoming. I might have to pass on that. I don't know how Harry can stand it."

DJ chuckled. "I guess he puts up with it because he's hopelessly in love with her."

"You're probably right about that. I've never known Harry to be so into a girl before. He's even getting a new Armani suit so he can be her escort when she's crowned queen next Friday. He is, of course, certain she will win."

"She's pretty certain too."

"Seems like her chances are pretty good." He paused. "So, you really don't mind me going to the game without you?"

"No. I'm actually really tired tonight."

"How about tomorrow? Want to do something?"

"Most of the day is pretty slammed for me." DJ told him about her early appointment. "And then I'll barely get home in time to make it to the fitting for the big fashion show."

"Why are you doing that?"

"My grandmother insists."

"She's going to make you model on crutches?"

"My physical therapist thinks I'll be down to a cane and walking cast by then."

"That's great."

"Yeah. Hopefully they can find an outfit that goes with this horrid shade of hospital blue."

He laughed. "Well, even with a cane and a cast, you'll still be the prettiest girl on the runway, DJ. Your grandmother probably knows that. She probably just wants to show you off."

DJ laughed so loudly that she actually snorted. Very attractive! "No, my grandmother doesn't hide her opinions when it comes to appearances. She would tell anyone who wanted to know that Taylor is the number-one beauty in this house."

"She obviously hasn't figured out that old saying that beauty is only skin deep, huh?" said Conner.

"Are you kidding? And her runner-up in the Carter House beauty contest would be Eliza."

"Well, no offense, DJ, but your grandmother has always struck me as a little nutty."

"You got that right." DJ leaned back on her bed and smiled. Conner seemed just like the same old Conner to her. Maybe her fears about Haley and him getting back together were nothing more than her own insecurities combined with her imagination—well, that plus Haley's wishful thinking. Anyway, DJ felt certain that she and Conner were just fine.

"I'll miss you tonight," he said finally.

"I'll miss you too."

"If you're not too wiped out from all your activities tomorrow, maybe we could go out."

"Sounds great," she told him. And she'd make sure she was up for it, even if she had to take an afternoon nap. "Have fun tonight."

"Get some rest."

She closed her phone and sighed. Maybe she would ask him about being exclusive tomorrow night. Not as in suggesting it, of course, but she would simply mention that someone had asked her and that she hadn't had an answer.

"Sounds like all is well in the ongoing romance of Conner and DJ," said Taylor.

"I didn't know you were lurking in the bathroom again," said DJ, sitting up to frown at her intrusive roommate.

"Lurking?" Taylor shook her head. "I thought I had the right to use that room just as much as you."

"Why don't you close the door when you're in there?"

"Because I was simply touching up my makeup, DJ. It's not like I need that much privacy to do my face. If you're so freaked about being overheard, maybe you should close the stupid door yourself. Or have your little sweetheart chats someplace else."

"Whatever." DJ leaned back into the pillows and exhaled loudly. "I'm too tired to fight with you anyway."

"And too tired to go out too?"

"Pretty much."

"I hope I'm never too tired to go out," said Taylor.

"Are you going out?"

"With Nick Jefferson."

DJ sat up and stared at Taylor. "Nick Jefferson is Madison Dormont's boyfriend."

"Ex-boyfriend."

"Since when?"

"Since . . ." She glanced at her watch. "Almost exactly an hour ago."

"Seriously?"

Taylor nodded with a smug look. "Nick heard Casey's little announcement this afternoon."

"And?"

"He told me that he had thought the website was bogus from the start." She pulled on what looked like a new red leather jacket. "Then he told me that he figured I would look way better than the body Casey had pasted to my head."

"He actually said *that*?"

She zipped up the jacket and grinned. "He did. Then he asked to meet me for coffee. Naturally, I told him that I had to return your car first."

"Naturally."

"So I came back, got my Vespa, and met him at McHenry's." Taylor did a last check of her hair, which as usual was perfect. "Anyway, we were just finishing up, and guess who walked in?"

It didn't take a genius to see where this was going. "Madison?"

"Yep. And she was furious."

DJ looked at the clock by her bed. It was 5:45. "And that must've been about 4:45 then? The time of the big breakup?"

"In front of witnesses too."

"And you're actually going out with him tonight?"

"Dinner, and then we'll make an appearance at the game."

"An appearance?"

"Well, I *am* running for homecoming queen, DJ. I should at least act like I'm interested in football, don't you think?"

"I think you've just given Madison the sympathy vote."

Taylor shrugged. "She can have it." Then she blew an air kiss at DJ. "Have a nice evening, little invalid."

"Thanks a lot." DJ made a face as Taylor made her exit. She didn't want to let it get to her, but sometimes that whole "invalid" thing stung. Even if this was only a temporary state, she thought Taylor could have a bit more empathy.

Finally, despite being tired, DJ decided to make the trip downstairs to see if anyone was interested in watching a DVD. But she quickly discovered that all the girls in Carter House were going out tonight. Rhiannon, the only straggler, informed DJ that Kriti had tagged along with Eliza and Harry to the game and that Casey had just left on a movie date with Garrison. And finally, that Rhiannon was actually going to hear a lecture with Josh Trundle.

"A lecture?" queried DJ.

"About early photography," Rhiannon told her. "We heard about it in journalism class, and we're both really into photography. He asked me to go, and I thought *why not?*"

"Good for you." DJ patted her on the back. She considered telling her that Taylor was going out with Nick Jefferson, which left Bradford wide open; but she suspected that Rhiannon wouldn't care one way or another anyway.

"It's not like this is a date." Rhiannon peered in the foyer mirror now, adjusting her brown velvet beret to a jaunty angle.

"No. No, of course, not." DJ nodded. "But, just so you know, I think Josh is sweet. It was interesting interviewing with him."

"Oh, yeah," Rhiannon said, "the article will be in the paper on Monday. It's too bad the paper takes so long to come out. It's usually old news by the time it's in print."

"Does anyone really read it?"

Rhiannon frowned. "Hopefully *somebody* reads it."

"Anyway, I got the impression that Josh is actually curious about God. I mean, in an offhanded sort of way."

"He claims to be an atheist, DJ."

"At least he's honest."

Rhiannon smiled. "But I have my own little theory about atheists."

"What's that?"

"I think they're just begging for someone to prove that God is real."

"You'd be the perfect one to do that."

"Oh, I don't think I can *prove* anything. But I can try to point him in the right direction."

"You go, girl."

By the time DJ made it down to dinner, now both tired and hungry, she was informed that, since everyone was going out,

Clara had been given the night off and Grandmother had gone out to dinner with her good friend the general.

"I fixed myself a microwave dinner," Inez told her, "and I plan to eat it in my room in front of the television—undisturbed."

"You don't have a TV in your room," DJ pointed out.

"Maybe not while you were there, but I do have one." Inez smiled slyly.

DJ went into the kitchen to forage for food. There were some leftovers, but nothing looked too appealing. What she was really craving was Hammerhead fish and chips. But she knew they didn't deliver. Maybe Conner would take her there tomorrow night. In the meantime, she would call out for pizza.

Of course, it ended up taking more than an hour for the delivery to be made. And when it came, it was not only cold, but tasted like the box it had been sitting in for too long. She ate a few slices anyway, and then she threw the rest of it away. She hoped Grandmother wouldn't spy the box and give her another lecture about fat and carbs. DJ knew the words by heart.

"Is that what you're wearing?" asked Grandmother when DJ finally made it back downstairs again. She'd just finished an exhausting physical therapy session when Grandmother had reminded her that the other girls had already gone to town for their fittings for the "big" fashion show and that DJ needed to go as well. As a result, DJ had hobbled up the stairs, freshened up a bit, then hurried back down. Now she was beat.

"I just finished my physical therapy," she said plainly, just in case Grandmother didn't remember that she'd been the one to drop her off and pick her up, complaining about the early hour for the Saturday appointment.

"But I thought the reason we came home was so you could change," persisted Grandmother. "Into something *respectable*."

"I'm tired, Grandmother. And in case you haven't noticed, I have a broken leg. And if you really insist on having me try on clothes, you're going to have to take me as is—sweats and all."

"Sweats." Grandmother wrinkled her nose. "Such an appropriate word for your attire."

"And easy to get off and on," pointed out DJ. "Much better for trying on clothes."

"Yes, yes. Well, let's get going then. The other girls are already there by now. I hope you don't mind that I let Taylor drive your car. That way she can give you a ride home. I will stay to meet with the fashion show committee. After the rehearsal we have some details to work out before next week."

Thanks to Grandmother's influence in the fashion world, several up-and-coming New York designers had donated clothing for the girls to wear, and The Chic Boutique had been selected as the retail host for the show. This was a change, as well as an upgrade, from the usual—Macy's. As a result, the local media sources were interested, and by the time DJ and Grandmother arrived cameras were shooting. The girls, particularly the homecoming queen candidates, seemed to be vying for camera time. DJ was surprised to see that Madison was there, but then there were about twenty girls altogether. Why wouldn't Madison and her friends be included? At the moment, Eliza was standing between Madison and Taylor, smiling directly into the camera lens as if she were imagining herself wearing the crown with her "court" surrounding her.

Taylor looked pleased with herself too, but Madison, although smiling, had a wicked look in her eye—like she was planning on tearing Taylor's hair out by the roots or perhaps slip a little arsenic into her water bottle. Hopefully there wouldn't be a serious cat fight today, although DJ suspected that might get the whole thing even more news time.

"And what do we have here?" asked Bonnie Hudson, as she moved toward DJ with the microphone. The cameras naturally followed, and suddenly DJ wished she had changed out of her sweats. "Surely, you don't plan to participate in the fashion show with a broken leg, do you?"

DJ laughed. "Well, my grandmother seems to think I should."

Bonnie did a quick recap of DJ's heroic rescue from last week. "And, tell us, DJ, how are you doing? Feeling a little better now?"

"A lot better, actually. My physical therapist told me that I can drive my car now. And I'll probably be off these crutches by the end of next week." DJ smiled into the camera.

"Yes," said Grandmother, pressing in next to DJ. "And that is exactly why we wanted to include her in this big fashion event." Then Grandmother did her best to publicize the fund-raiser, listing the names of the designers. "They are allowing us to wear the same clothing that was on the runway last spring—their fall fashion lineup. We are very fortunate."

Bonnie nodded then turned back to DJ. "So, DJ, since you plan to be crutch-free by the end of next week, does that mean you'll be at the Crescent Cove High homecoming too? Your friends were just telling us about it. Do you plan to attend the festivities and the dance?"

DJ laughed again. "I might go to the dance, but I doubt that I'll be doing much dancing. If I'm able to walk without crutches, it will involve a cane and a walking boot. Not exactly a graceful setup."

Bonnie smiled. "Well, we're just glad to see you're doing well. And, once again, we wish you the best."

Soon the media was on its way to a car wreck on a nearby interstate, and the girls were inside The Chic Boutique, which was closed for regular business. Voices were being raised as twenty Crescent Cove High School girls now competed for clothes.

DJ, of course, knew that this wasn't only about clothes.

DJ and Madison reached for the same red dress. "Just because you hogged the media," Madison snapped, "doesn't mean you get to hog the best clothes too."

DJ was pretty sure that she'd reached first, but she pulled her hand back just the same. No way was she going to get into it with Madison. Not with a broken leg and cracked ribs. "Sorry," she said casually. "I was just looking for something that would be easy to try on over my walking cast."

"Excuse me," said Eliza as she snatched the hanger from Madison's hand. "But DJ gets first pick today."

"Says who?" Madison turned and glared at Eliza now.

"That's okay, Eliza," said DJ quickly. She thought she could see actual smoke shooting out of Madison's nostrils now. "She can have it."

"No, she can't," said Eliza in a pleasant but firm voice. She pushed the red dress toward DJ. "Go and try this on."

Madison stepped directly in front of Eliza now. "Look, Miss I'm-So-Sweet-Southern-Belle, I don't know what makes you think you rule the world or that you can take over our town and our school and everything, but some of us are getting sick and tired of you and the rest of your *Carter House girls*."

Eliza blinked. "Well, now, Madison. Let's not lose our heads over a silly little red dress."

Madison grabbed the dress, pulling it so hard that DJ heard a tear.

"What's going on here?" demanded Louise Bristow. She was part of the fashion show committee and a friend of Grandmother's.

"I think Madison is in a bad mood today," said Eliza innocently. "DJ had picked up this dress first. She thought it would be easy to put on because of her broken leg and all. Madison got angry because she wanted the dress for herself. And now she has just torn it."

Louise scowled at Madison. "Let me see the dress."

Madison handed it over.

Louise adjusted her glasses and peered closely at the dress then shook her head. "Madison Dormont, you *have* torn this dress!" Now Louise held the dress in the air and called out loudly. "Girls, girls, everyone needs to be quiet and listen to me for a moment. Most of the clothes you will be wearing are design originals. Isn't that correct, Katherine?"

Grandmother nodded. "Yes. Very expensive design originals. As I already mentioned, they were part of Fall Fashion Week, which was held last spring."

"And you need to handle them with care," said Louise. "Madison Dormont, in an ugly display of temper, has damaged a dress. What do you have to say for yourself?"

All eyes were on Madison now, but she just glowered at them with her arms folded across her chest and said nothing.

"Well!" Louise looked seriously angry now. "I am therefore dismissing Madison from the fashion show," she declared. Several gasps were heard, and then Louise continued. "Let this be a warning to all of you. If you girls cannot get along, and if you cannot act like ladies, you will not be part of this show. Is that perfectly clear?"

The boutique owner unlocked the front door, and with a dark frown for Madison, she waited for the angry girl to stomp out of the shop. "There," she said as she closed and locked the door then made a pretense of brushing off her hands. "Good riddance of bad rubbish."

Some of the girls laughed, but others—particularly Madison's friends—looked around uncomfortably. And before long they all returned to selecting clothes, with a bit more care now.

"I see a scene with pig's blood coming for someone," DJ said under her breath to Taylor.

"Hey, we should watch that movie tonight," said Taylor.

"Sounds good," said DJ, "but I have a date."

"Oh, right." Taylor picked up a slinky black top and examined it more closely.

It took a while, but finally it seemed that everyone had at least one outfit. Some of the girls, like Eliza and Taylor, had three outfits. This had been Grandmother's doing. She hoped to get them a little exposure for next weekend. DJ got to beg off with just one, saying that it would take her forever just to change into that. She had decided on a sophisticated camel-colored cashmere knit dress. "It doesn't really go with this," she teased as she held the dress above her blue boot. "But maybe I can get some brown spray paint and give the boot a makeover."

When they were done with the fitting and practicing walking the runway at the historic Keller Tavern where the fashion show would take place the next Saturday, Taylor drove DJ home. Casey had gone next door to Starbucks to meet Garrison. DJ thought Taylor was acting slightly odd, like something was wrong.

"So, how was your date with Nick last night?" asked DJ, hoping to find out what was bugging her.

"Great. I like him. He likes me."

"I'm glad that Madison didn't get to lay her claws into you today. She looked like she had murder on her mind."

"Someone should tell that girl that anger is unbecoming in a homecoming queen candidate."

"Yeah, I'd nominate someone like you to do that."

Now there was a lull in the conversation, and DJ wondered once again if something was troubling Taylor. It wasn't like her to be this quiet. Not without the radio or CD player going.

"Uh, DJ?" Taylor finally broke the silence, but her voice sounded slightly odd now. Almost as if she were being sympathetic and very un-Taylor like.

"Huh?"

"I want to tell you something, except that I really don't."

"What do you mean?"

"I mean, it's about Conner ..."

"What about Conner?"

"He was at the game last night."

"I know."

"With Haley."

DJ bit her lip as she tried to wrap her head around this bit of news. "You mean Haley was at the game and Conner was at the game? Like they met up there and sat together?"

"Not exactly. More like they *came* together. They *sat* together. And they *left* together."

"Oh." DJ imagined Conner and Haley ... together at the game ... and after the game ... and she didn't like what she was seeing.

"I know that you think I'm the Queen of Mean and that I'd really get a kick out of hurting you, but that's not true."

"I don't think that."

"I just thought you should know."

"Yeah." DJ felt a lump growing in her throat. "Did you see anything else? I mean, that you think I should know about?"

Taylor didn't answer. She pressed her lips together and looked straight ahead.

"What?"

"I saw them kissing in the parking lot before they got into his pickup."

CONNER WAS AT CARTER HOUSE when Taylor and DJ pulled up. His pickup was parked in front, and he was sitting on the porch steps, with his head literally hanging.

"I'm going in the back door," said Taylor as she gave DJ the keys. Then she got DJ's crutches from the backseat and set them next to the opened passenger door, pausing to put a hand on DJ's shoulder. "Hang in there, invalid girl."

DJ just nodded then slowly got out of the car, slowly put the crutches into place, and slowly made her way to the front porch. Conner was standing now. His hands were shoved in his pockets and his head was still hanging. DJ knew what was coming.

"We need to talk," he said as she slowly approached him.

"I know." She nodded and paused on the walk. "And I want to make this quick, okay?"

He seemed confused now. "Sure, okay."

"You're a great guy, Conner," she began, determined to hold back the tears that felt just seconds away. "And I really like you. But it's not really working anymore. And I think it's time to break up."

He blinked. "You want to break up?"

She nodded, swallowing against what felt like a rock in her throat. "I think it's for the best. Don't you?"

He nodded now too. "Someone told you about Haley and me, about seeing us together last night, didn't they?"

She just shrugged. "It doesn't matter, Conner. Haley is a sweet girl. And you guys were together long before I came along. And—" She knew that she couldn't go on without crying. "So, I just think it's for the best. I need to go in now."

He moved, and she slowly made her way past him, slowly clumped up the stairs, and after what seemed like several years, finally made it to her room, which was thankfully vacant. Even the bathroom was vacant. Then DJ threw down her crutches, fell down on her bed, and cried.

Monday came too soon. DJ had had a day and a half to recover. Or to try to. Everyone at Carter House had been very nice and understanding. Even Grandmother, although DJ had no idea if she knew what was going on.

Now DJ had to face the real world. Her plan was to put on a happy face and pretend like all was well. She'd already told her friends that she had broken up with Conner. And it was the truth. She'd also gone to church with Rhiannon yesterday. And, it wasn't easy, but she was doing her best to trust God with the whole thing. Like Rhiannon kept reminding her, "The heavenly Father knows best." DJ hoped that was true.

"You sure you want to drive today?" asked Taylor after they were all in the car.

"Are you worried I can't do it?" DJ stuck the key in the ignition.

"No," said Taylor quickly.

Casey had already nabbed the passenger seat. And probably because Taylor was still feeling sorry for DJ, she didn't even make a fuss about it.

"By the way, I won't need a ride home after school," said Taylor.

DJ just nodded and turned the key.

Casey attempted small talk, even telling them that she and Rhiannon were going in to see the drug counselor after school. "I'll have to miss volleyball practice," she said. "But I guess it's worth it."

"Of course it's worth it," said Taylor.

"Good for you for following through," added DJ.

Somehow DJ made it through the day. She smiled and joked and acted like everything was fine. She skimmed over the article about her in the school paper, wincing slightly at the photo where she still looked kind of beat up.

She'd spotted Conner only once all day long, and that was in passing. Thankfully he hadn't been with Haley. After school, DJ wasn't too surprised when Haley didn't offer her a ride to the pool. Not that it mattered, since DJ had her own car back. Actually, DJ was tempted to give up swimming, just to avoid Haley, but her therapist had mentioned how much stronger her leg was getting and how the swimming was certainly speeding her recovery. So DJ decided to tough it out.

To her relief, Haley wasn't anywhere to be seen at the pool. She'd probably done the early morning practice instead. Well, that served her right. Haley had told DJ that she didn't like getting up that early, but it seemed fair that she should sacrifice something for taking Conner away from her. Or had she just taken him back? Did it even matter?

"Hey, DJ," said Caleb as he climbed down from the lifeguard stand to help with her crutches again. "It looks like you're moving a little faster."

She kind of shrugged. "I guess . . ."

"Feeling down?"

"I guess I'm just getting fed up with all this." Naturally, she couldn't tell him about Conner. Let him assume it was simply her physical condition.

"Don't worry. It won't be too long before this is just a memory." He grinned. "Hey, I saw you on the news."

She rolled her eyes. "Yeah. My grandmother was furious at me for going slumming that day. Who knew I was going to be on TV?"

"I thought you looked cute." He winked. "And much prettier than those plastic-looking girls running for homecoming queen."

She laughed as she eased herself into the water. "I'll be sure and send them your regards."

"Have a good swim."

All that week DJ wore her happy face and went to classes and acted normal—even more friendly than usual. And when she felt discouraged, she tried to remember to pray.

But by Thursday afternoon, she was down. Really down. She knew she was just feeling sorry for herself, but it seemed that everyone except her had a life. Taylor and Eliza were still duking it out for homecoming queen—and Madison was being more unpleasant than ever, mostly to Taylor and Eliza. DJ thought everyone in the school must be sick of the whole election by now. Eliza probably had the title in the bag, not that anyone really cared. DJ just hoped that Madison didn't arrange to have a bucket of pig's blood dumped over Eliza's head. Or worse. Perhaps Eliza's daddy should hire a body-guard for the weekend.

But the last straw for DJ was seeing Conner and Haley in an embrace next to his red pickup. It felt like someone had twisted the knife in her back as she realized how happy they were together. And even though she prayed as she drove to her physical therapy appointment, she didn't feel much better when she got there. And as she went through the exercises and even practiced walking with a cane, she felt like crying.

"You seem a little down today," said Selena. "I thought you'd be a little more excited about getting off the crutches."

"I am," said DJ in a flat voice. "But I guess I'm just sick of everything. Sick of hurting, sick of being left out, sick of being incapacitated."

Selena nodded as she adjusted a strap on DJ's new walking boot — black this time. DJ knew she should be glad about that; but the truth was she didn't care. She didn't really care about anything.

"As you know, this is our last session, DJ." Selena stood and placed her hands on her hips. "You'll continue with the exercises at home, but you won't need to come in here again."

DJ nodded. "Yeah. Thanks for everything, Selena. You've been great."

Selena smiled. "I wasn't fishing for compliments. But before I sign you out for good, I have one last exercise for you."

"What?"

Selena handed DJ a card with a name and an address written down. "Who's Lacy Michaels?" asked DJ.

"Your final therapist."

"Do I need an appointment?"

"I'll call and let her know that you're on your way."

"Now?"

"Yes, now." Selena glanced at the big clock. "I'm letting you out twenty minutes early anyway, so I know you have the time. It's less than three minutes from here."

DJ thanked her again and drove over to what turned out to be the Ronald McDonald House, across from the hospital. It seemed weird to be without her crutches, and walking with a cane was awkward.

"I'm here to see Lacy Michaels," she told the woman who opened the door.

"There she is," said the woman, nodding to where a girl was sitting at a table coloring a picture of a horse.

"Are you DJ?" The girl smiled brightly at her.

"I am. Are you Lacy?" DJ was confused.

The girl stood and shook DJ's hand. "Selena said you needed to talk to me about something."

DJ wasn't sure what to say. So she sat down and picked up a crayon. She knew that Ronald McDonald House was for kids who were sick. Did that mean that Lacy was sick? She looked okay.

"Do you have Ewing's Sarcoma?" Lacy asked.

"What?"

"Bone cancer."

"No." DJ looked down at her leg. "You mean because of the walking cast?"

Lacy nodded.

"No. I broke my leg."

Lacy brightened. "Oh, you're that girl who saved that little boy, the one who was in the news, aren't you?"

"Yeah, that's me." DJ smiled.

Lacy looked confused. "So why did Selena send you to talk to me?"

194

DJ considered this. "Do you have—I can't remember the name—but do you have bone cancer?"

"I'm in remission." Lacy stood now and pulled up her jeans to reveal a prosthetic leg made of metal and plastic. "They had to amputate my leg when I was six. That was five years ago. I come in for checkups once a year."

DJ felt foolish. Obviously, Selena had sent her here in an effort to nip this little pity party in the bud. "So, how are you feeling now?"

"Really great." Lacy grinned.

"Why are you here at Ronald McDonald House?"

"My mom and I stayed here when I went through my treatments—because it's a long drive to the hospital from our house. Now we just spend the night here when I come for checkups. The people here are so nice. It's always fun to see them."

"That's a pretty horse." DJ pointed to the picture. "You're a good artist."

"Thanks. That's Dandy, but he's not mine."

"Whose is he?"

"He lives at Sunshine Stables, the place where I take riding lessons."

"You take riding lessons?"

"Dressage. That's like English."

"Oh." DJ thought about this one-legged girl learning to ride a horse.

"My mom said I can get a horse of my own when I'm twelve." Lacy giggled. "I used to be worried that I wasn't going to make it to be twelve. But this morning the doctor told me I might get to be one hundred and twelve."

"Do you think you'll still be riding a horse then?"

Lacy laughed. "Yeah, I hope so."

"Well, you're an inspiration, Lacy."

"Why?"

"Because I was feeling sorry for myself for having a broken leg."

Lacy smiled knowingly. "That's probably why Selena sent you to talk to me. I've talked to lots of kids about this stuff. I guess it's kind of like therapy for me too."

DJ nodded, feeling totally pathetic.

"Can I have your autograph?" Lacy tore the picture of the horse from the tablet then pushed the blank tablet toward DJ.

"Sure, but I don't know why."

"Because you're famous."

DJ picked up the red crayon and scrawled "DJ Lane" across the paper and handed it back. In the meantime, Lacy had written "To DJ" on top of the horse picture and "Love, Lacy" at the bottom. "Here," she told her. "This is for you."

"Thanks!"

"Are you going to be okay?" Lacy's pale eyebrows drew together with concern.

DJ grinned. "Yeah, I'm going to be great." They both stood, and DJ hugged Lacy. "Thanks for helping me."

"You're welcome. My mom says that I would make a good counselor someday."

"Your mom is right." Then DJ told her good-bye and slowly headed back out. Still, she felt strangely encouraged as she drove across town toward home. She felt sorry for Lacy—well, *sorry* wasn't the right word. She felt some kind of empathy for the girl. And yet Lacy said she felt great. She really was an inspiration. And as DJ pulled into the driveway at Carter House, she was determined to learn from Lacy. Whether it was feeling sorry for herself for getting hurt by a car or hurt by a boyfriend, DJ was determined to have no more pity parties!

"You're not going to believe this," said Rhiannon. DJ was on her way to U.S. History, her last class before lunch. And, still not used to walking with the cane, her leg was aching and she wasn't moving too fast.

"Can it wait?" asked DJ. "I'm running late." Then she laughed. "Okay, I'm not exactly *running* anywhere, but I am late."

"I'll walk and talk," said Rhiannon as she went alongside her. "You just listen."

"Okay."

"Someone has decided to run a write-in campaign for you."

DJ stopped walking now. She turned and stared at Rhiannon. "What?"

"For homecoming queen."

DJ groaned. "Why?"

"Probably because people like you, DJ. And maybe they're sick of the other options."

DJ laughed and started walking again. "Like I'd even have a chance. The votes are supposed to be cast during lunch, right?"

"Right. But the word is spreading like wildfire. I can't believe you didn't hear about it yourself."

"Well, it's a crazy idea, but I guess there's nothing I can do about, right?"

"I don't see how. But I thought you should know. And I didn't want you to hear it from Eliza. She's not too happy."

"Oh, great. She's in my next class."

"I know."

"And Taylor too." DJ frowned at the door to the classroom. Rhiannon patted her on the back. "Good luck."

DJ hadn't even gone through the door before Eliza accosted her, pulling her off to one side of the hallway. "You're not going to go through with it, are you?"

"What?"

"Being a write-in!"

DJ just shrugged. "It wasn't my idea."

Eliza smiled hopefully. "So, you'll put a stop to it then?"

"How?"

"I don't know. Go on the radio and tell everyone that you're not interested."

Now DJ felt offended. "Why wouldn't I be interested?"

Eliza looked sheepish. "Well, you're not, are you? I mean, here you are with your cane and your big funny boot. Surely you don't want to be homecoming queen looking like *that*."

Something about the way Eliza said "that" just got to DJ. And suddenly, for no rational or explainable reason, DJ wanted to run as a write-in. Even if it was just to rock Eliza's world. She smiled and began walking again.

"You're not going to stop it?" Eliza frowned.

"I don't see how I can."

"But my parents are here. They came to see me crowned."

"And they probably will see you crowned, Eliza." DJ put a hand on her shoulder. "Seriously, what chance would I have against you?"

Eliza nodded. "Yes. You're probably right."

"So, chill, okay? We're late for class."

Of course, DJ found it impossible to think about history, U.S. or otherwise. All she could think was—how had this happened? Who had launched this crazy write-in campaign? And should she be flattered, or should she be scared? What if it was something Madison had schemed up, a prank? And suddenly, it seemed that had to be it. Madison was trying to split the vote. She wanted DJ to steal votes from Eliza enabling Madison to win.

As soon as class was over, DJ looked for Eliza. But she'd already taken off. Probably off to get more votes.

"I heard the news," said Taylor as she came and walked alongside DJ. "Congrats."

"You don't mind?"

"Are you kidding? I think it's cool."

"Well, I don't," said DJ, trying to walk fast, which seemed hopeless. "I just figured it out. Madison is behind this. She wants to split the vote so she can win."

Taylor laughed. "That's not a bad theory, but it's all wet."

"How do you know?"

"I have ears."

"Huh?"

"I've heard people talking. The write-in is because of you, DJ. People like you, and they're not too fond of the other candidates. If you ask me, you've got the best chance of winning." She grinned and slapped DJ on the back. "I know I'm voting for you."

"No way!"

Taylor nodded and winked. "Oh, yeah. Way." Then she hurried off toward the cafeteria where ballots would be collected.

Several people came up to DJ as she hobbled like an old woman toward the cafeteria. Some wished her luck. Some said they were voting for her. No one seemed to think it was a bad idea. Still, DJ knew better than to get her hopes up. That was crazy. By the end of the day, she'd probably get a handful of votes—the sympathy votes. But then it would be over. And she would be glad.

"We have breaking news," said Garrison's smooth voice over the school loudspeaker. It was last period, and DJ was in the locker room folding towels. She had PE, but since she wasn't able to participate in class yet she was given oddball tasks. "The votes have been counted, and although the final outcome will not be revealed until the big game tonight, there has been a successful write-in candidate who will now be part of the homecoming court. Congratulations, DJ Lane—*you are a contender!* See you all at the game tonight. Go, Mighty Maroons!"

All the girls in the locker room cheered, and soon they were coming over to congratulate her.

Taylor didn't cheer, she got serious. "We need to go shopping," Taylor said.

"Shopping?"

"Oh yeah. You need a dress for tonight."

"But I was going to swim—I promised my therapist I'd do three days a week."

Taylor frowned. "But you need a gown."

"This is crazy."

"Crazy like a fox." Taylor grinned now. "I have a plan. I'll drive you to the pool and take your car to do some scouting."

"Scouting?"

"For a gown."

"Oh."

"I'll pick you up at four thirty. Can you be ready by then?"

"I guess."

Taylor dropped DJ at the pool. "You be out here at four thirty," she said. "Don't be late."

DJ promised. Her head was still spinning from this strange development. She wondered if she really had to go through with it. But then she thought of everyone who had congratulated her. She thought of kids who'd said things like, "Wouldn't it be cool if a nice, normal girl won this year?" She thought of the girls in PE and friends on the volleyball team—all who'd been happy for her. Could she really let them down?

"Congratulations, DJ," said Haley as DJ hobbled across the deck with her cane.

DJ blinked in surprise. "Uh, yeah, thanks."

"That's really cool." Haley nodded. "I voted for you too."

"Wow, thanks."

"Uh, I was wondering, do you have an escort?"

"An escort?"

"You know. All the candidates are supposed to have an escort."

DJ frowned.

"I thought it could be a problem. And, okay, please, don't think this is crazy, but what about Conner?"

DJ stared at her, and then shook her head in a firm *no*.

"I mean he still really likes you. And he misses you too."

"Really?"

"I could ask him for you."

"No, thanks." DJ shook her head again.

"Okay. I guess it was dumb."

"No," said DJ. "It was sweet. And, okay, kinda dumb too."

Haley grinned.

DJ made her way to the lane on the end, but today Caleb wasn't around to help her. She didn't really need so much help now that the crutches were gone, and her leg seemed stronger too — still, she missed him. She set her cane beneath the lifeguard chair and carefully climbed down the ladder. As she swam she considered her new dilemma. An escort. She wondered if Taylor would have a suggestion for that too. DJ ran possibilities through her head, but she honestly couldn't think of one guy she wanted to ask.

"Hey," said Caleb as DJ slowly climbed up the ladder. He had her cane in hand. "Congratulations!"

"Who told *you* about it?" she asked with surprise.

"About what?" He handed her the cane.

"The election?"

"What election?"

She laughed. "Maybe we should start over." She held up her cane. "Is this what you were congratulating me about?"

He nodded and scratched his head. "What did you think I meant?"

So she quickly recapped the last half of her day. And now he congratulated her again. "That's fantastic, DJ. Very, very cool."

"I guess. Except that now I'm scrambling. My roommate is taking me formal shopping in a few minutes and somehow I need to find an escort."

Caleb put his hand across his mid section and made a formal bow. Then, standing, he smiled. "Escort, at your service, miss."

"Are you serious?"

"Why not?"

"You'd do that for me?"

"And for me too. I think it sounds fun."

She frowned. "You're supposed to wear a suit, I think."

"I happen to have a dark brown suit."

She blinked and shook her head. "This is like a weird dream." Then she remembered the Steven King movie. "But I hope it doesn't involve a bucket of pig's blood."

He laughed. "I've seen *Carrie* too. But I don't think you need to be worried."

She told him where to pick her up and when then hobbled off to try on dresses. After three dresses, she wanted to give up. She was exhausted and frustrated.

"Try this one," Taylor said. It was a plum-colored satin gown. "It will look nice with Caleb's brown suit."

"Okay, but it's the last one I'm trying on. So it better look good."

It did. It looked stunning. Even DJ had to admit that.

"And since you can wear only one shoe, you better go with your black ballet slipper," Taylor said. "Let's go home and get ready."

Back home Eliza was not a bit pleased when she saw DJ. In fact, she wasn't even speaking to her. Neither was Kriti.

"Don't worry about them," said Rhiannon as she helped DJ with her hair.

"I'll be glad when this is all over with," said Taylor with a bored expression. She was putting eye shadow on. When her own makeup was finished and perfect as usual, she offered to help DJ with hers. DJ happily accepted. Just as they were finishing up, Inez knocked on the door and before anyone could answer, she stuck her head in.

"Your young man is downstairs," she told DJ with a wry expression, "talking to your grandmother."

"Oh, dear," said DJ, hurrying to wrap around her shoulders the faux fur cape that Taylor had loaned her. "I better hurry."

"No telling what your Grandmother might be saying to him," teased Taylor.

"She wasn't happy when I told her how old he was," admitted DJ.

But once downstairs, she saw that Grandmother was smiling and seemed completely pleased with DJ's escort.

"You didn't tell me that Caleb was a Bennett, Desiree."

"Desiree?" Caleb's brows lifted curiously.

"DJ is fine," DJ said.

"I've known the Bennetts for ages," continued Grandmother. "A very fine family indeed."

DJ smiled nervously at Caleb. "Ready to go?" she asked hopefully. If they stuck around much longer, her grandmother might try to arrange their marriage.

"Not until I give you this." Caleb shyly produced a wrist corsage. "The florist seemed to think these were still acceptable."

"And it's the school colors," pointed out Rhiannon.

Finally, good-byes were said and Grandmother even wished her good luck. But by the time she was sitting in Caleb's car, she was a bundle of nerves.

"I know I shouldn't care so much," she admitted.

"Why not?" he asked.

"Because it's never been my dream to do something like this. I've never liked this kind of attention. And now here I am." She shook her head. "It's so unbelievable. Like a fairy tale to even be included in the court." DJ was glad she'd remembered to put on two layers of antiperspirant.

"Well, I hope you get crowned queen tonight," said Caleb after he parked the car near the stadium and helped her out. "But whether or not you win, you are a winner. Everyone can see that."

"That's nice of you to say." She took his arm and adjusted her cane. "But I don't feel like much of a winner." The truth was she felt ridiculous as she limped across the parking lot. But several kids called out to her, wishing her good luck and saying they'd voted for her.

"Thanks," she called back, feeling a bit more confident.

Before long, the court was assigned cars that would be driven in parade fashion around the track. To DJ's surprise she and Caleb were picked to ride in a very cool Bentley convertible that Eliza had been eyeing for herself.

"Nice wheels," called out Taylor as she waved from the back of an old Mercedes convertible.

"Thanks," said DJ. "Good luck!"

But Taylor just winked and grinned as the procession began.

"You ready for this?" asked Caleb as he gave her hand a warm squeeze.

DJ sat up straighter (remembering her grandmother's constant reminders about good posture) then smiled. "I think so."

With the band playing loudly, the classic cars paraded around the bend of the track then one by one pulled forward in front of the large podium that was decorated with crepe paper and flowers. DJ couldn't help but notice how fantastic both Eliza and Taylor looked tonight, but there was nothing unusual about that. Even Madison looked pretty good, and she was smiling brightly as if she had the sweetest disposition of them all.

Suddenly DJ wondered who would win. Eliza seemed most likely—and she would make a beautiful homecoming queen. But then Madison had a lot of friends too. And Taylor had a lot of male admirers who could've cast their votes in her direction.

Now the principal was making his way to the podium. He looked odd and out of place in his tuxedo, but he soon warmed up the audience with some cheerful banter about homecoming and traditions and how Crescent Cove was such a great little town.

"And now for the moment you've all been waiting for," he said dramatically. Then he paused to turn and look at the members of the court still seated in the backs of the classic convertibles. "Have you ever seen such a beautiful bunch of ladies?" The crowd cheered, and then he went on to introduce the girls. DJ felt like she was going to burst if he didn't get this over with soon. Still, she just smiled, sitting up straight and grasping Caleb's hand tightly.

"And this year's homecoming queen is ..." He paused for a drum roll. "Desiree Jeannette Lane—otherwise known as *DJ Lane*!" At this moment, DJ felt a shock wave running through her, from the roots of her hair to the tips of her toes, and she wondered if this was for real or if she'd imagined the whole thing. But when she turned to look at Caleb, he was nodding and smiling. "Congratulations, Queen DJ."

And while he was helping her out of the car and waiting for her to get her cane into place—to her amazement—the crowd was going wild. Clapping and yelling things like "Way to go, DJ!"

As Caleb helped her toward the podium, she turned and smiled at the rest of the court—all of them. And they all smiled back. But DJ felt sure she saw traces of shock and disappointment behind some of their smiles. Well, except for Taylor. Her smile looked wide and genuine, and she gave DJ a big thumb's-up.

"Congratulations, Desiree Jeannette," said the principal when, with Caleb's help, she finally reached the top of the podium. Then the principal handed her a bouquet of red roses as last year's queen arranged the crown on top of DJ's head. Then she too congratulated her and stepped aside.

Now the principal chuckled into the mike. "But your friends call you DJ, right?"

DJ nodded and smiled, unsure of what she was supposed to do. "Thank you!" she told him, and then she turned to the crowd which was still clapping and cheering. "Thank you, everyone!" she cried out. "Thank you so much! This is unbelievable. Thank you!"

"So, DJ, do you have an acceptance speech?" he asked as he pointed the mike toward her.

She blinked. "Well, no. I just want to say thanks again to everyone. This is so amazing. I think I'm in shock."

The principal nodded and smiled. "Well, I just happen to have a small speech prepared, if DJ doesn't mind." He glanced at her, and she nodded eagerly.

Then he cleared his throat and unfolded a piece of paper. "Some of you might be aware that DJ recently became known as the hometown heroine when she saved a young boy's life." He smiled at her. "And, naturally, we were all very proud of her. We're also proud of her for her athletic achievements, although her injuries have temporarily benched her. But another thing that some of you grown-ups might not have heard is that DJ was a write-in candidate for homecoming queen. Not only that, but she's somewhat new to our town, so winning this crown is quite an achievement." He paused and smiled at her again. "But here's something about DJ that some of you younger folks may not be aware of, and something that some of you older ones may have forgotten: DJ's mother, the late Elizabeth Carter Lane, was crowned Crescent Cove High's homecoming queen too. Back in 1976, DJ's mother ruled this podium. And today the crown is passed on to her daughter. Hey, DJ, I'll bet your mother is watching and cheering for you right now. Congratulations!"

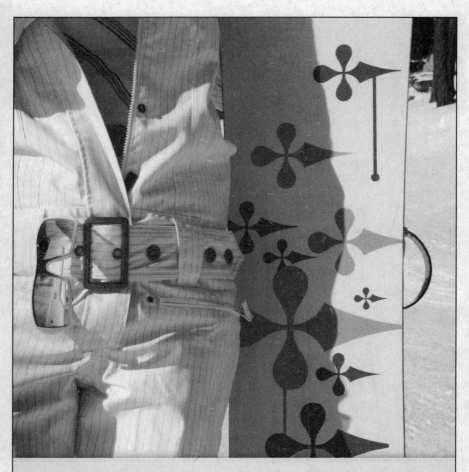

viva vermont!

carter house girls

meLODy
caRLson

bestselling author

Read chapter 1 of *Viva Vermont!*,
Book 4 in Carter House Girls.

DJ STILL FELT LIKE CINDERELLA the next morning—
Cinderella after the magic was gone, that is. Not that she wasn't
still pumped about last night. Who would've thought that she,
of all people, would be crowned homecoming queen? But now
it was Saturday morning, and her grandmother was droning
on and on about today's BIG fashion show, like she thought
they were walking a runway in Paris instead of Crescent Cove,
Connecticut.

"And I expect my girls to behave themselves as ladies,"
Grandmother said as the six girls poked at their breakfast of
granola, fresh fruit, and plain yogurt. For no explainable reason, DJ was craving bacon, eggs, and pancakes slathered in
butter and syrup. Like that was going to happen.

"You will be representing Carter House ... and me," continued Grandmother. "And this fashion show is your debut in

the community. I expect all of you to put your very best foot forward."

"That would be my right foot." DJ held up her cane and frowned down at her large walking cast. "Do I still have to do this, Grandmother? My leg is really aching today."

"That's because you were such a show-off last night." Eliza's tone was teasing, but DJ sensed a hard glint in her pretty blue eyes.

"You're just jealous," said Taylor as she refilled her coffee cup.

"I most certainly am not," said Eliza, her chin held high. "I couldn't be happier for DJ. I thought it was just the sweetest thing ever seeing her limping forward with her cute little cane to receive the crown. Even my parents were glad for her."

Casey made a snorting laugh of disbelief, and Grandmother gave her a stern look. "Sorry," said Casey sarcastically. "But I happened to have been sitting directly behind Eliza's parents last night, and I heard her mother gasp when they announced DJ's name over the loudspeaker."

Eliza blinked. "Well, that's only because she was surprised."

Grandmother cleared her throat. "We were all rather surprised to see Desiree crowned queen last night." Then she actually smiled at DJ, in a way that made DJ wonder if Grandmother had been just a little bit pleased.

"I wasn't surprised," said Rhiannon. "It was the buzz at school yesterday."

"The buzz?" Eliza frowned. "Like who even uses that word anymore?"

Rhiannon just shrugged, and Casey looked like she wanted to say something that would probably get her excused from the table. Instead, Grandmother continued her monologue about the fashion show.

"Well, I'm sure you must all be ready to put the homecoming queen competition behind you now, girls. We need to focus on today's big event. I want you all to be at your very best." She pointed a finger at DJ. "And, yes, Desiree, I certainly do expect you to participate today. After all, this show is part of the Crescent Cove Homecoming weekend. The alumni would certainly appreciate seeing this year's reigning queen amongst the models. Take some pain medication if you need to. Besides, you only have one outfit to show, how hard can that be? Really, I don't think it's too much to expect you to contribute your best effort. This is, after all, for a very good cause."

"What very good cause?" asked DJ.

Grandmother frowned. "Well, I don't recall offhand, but I do know it's something worthwhile." She glanced up at the clock on the sideboard. "And we need to be at Keller Tavern by eleven."

"Keller Tavern?" questioned Casey. "Will they be serving beer?"

Grandmother gave Casey a withering look. "No. For your information, Keller Tavern is a historic inn that dates back more than two hundred years, and it is merely the finest restaurant in this part of Connecticut."

"So, no beer then . . ." Taylor exchanged a smirk with Casey, and DJ wondered if those two were actually starting to get along again.

"Anyway," said Grandmother loudly, "I'm sure you girls will want to spend plenty of time in preparation. Makeup, nails, hair . . . all must be absolute perfection."

"Why nails?" asked DJ as she peered at her hands. "I mean, who's going to see our nails?"

"I'm sure that I've already mentioned that I expect some very important fashion people to be in attendance at this event." Grandmother stood stiffly. She was clearly getting impatient. "And I want you girls to look divine." She smiled directly at Taylor and Eliza now. "You just never know. Some of you girls may be scouted for some other important fashion projects. You must always be ready for the unexpected." Grandmother smiled and patted her silver hair.

"And if you'll excuse me, I want to be sure that I am looking my best as well." With narrow eyes, she peered at all of them. "So, do not be late, girls. I expect to see you all at Keller Tavern at eleven sharp. Until then."

"*Until then*," said DJ in an affected voice, but only after Grandmother was out of earshot.

"So, you guys aren't actually taking this seriously?" asked Casey. She seemed to be directing this to Eliza and Taylor.

"What?" asked Eliza.

"I mean modeling professionally." Casey rolled her eyes. "You're not really into it, are you?"

"Why not?" asked Taylor. "I hear the money is pretty good."

"It's not about the money," said Eliza in a superior tone. Easy for her to say since her family was one of the wealthiest in the country. "I simply think it would be fun."

"What do your parents think?" asked DJ.

Eliza shrugged. "They think that it's nice that I'm learning to be a *lady*." She sort of laughed. "But I doubt they'd be too excited to see me taking modeling as seriously as your grandmother does. Still, I think it would be kind of exciting."

"I'd take it seriously," said Kriti. Then she frowned. "If I wasn't so short."

"You could still do print," said Eliza. She used her forefingers and thumbs to frame Kriti's face. "You would be great for cosmetic ads. They go for those exotic-looking girls."

Placated, Kriti smiled.

"Well, the only part of the fashion industry that interests me is design," said Rhiannon as she stood and pushed her chair in. "And I consider myself fortunate to have Mrs. Carter's influence to help me get where I'm going."

"And don't underestimate that influence," said Eliza. "My mother told me last night that Mrs. Carter still has some pretty impressive connections in both New York and Paris."

Taylor chuckled. "Yeah. Ms. Katherine Carter may be getting long in the tooth, but the old girl's not dead yet."

"We better get moving," said Eliza.

DJ groaned as she stood and reached for her cane. Her leg really was aching today. This fashion show might be a great big deal to some girls, but to DJ it was simply a great big pain. Everyone began heading for their rooms. But, as usual of late, DJ moved more slowly, clomping along like an old woman with her cane and big boot. When she finally reached the foot of the stairs, Eliza seemed to be waiting for her.

Eliza smiled stiffly at DJ as she placed a hand on her shoulder. "You know . . . despite what Casey or the others might say, I really was happy for you last night."

DJ blinked at her. "Seriously?"

"I really did think it was *sweet*."

Sweet? That word put DJ's teeth on edge. "You actually seemed kind of shocked at the time."

"Well, naturally, it was pretty surprising." Eliza flipped a silky blonde strand of hair over her shoulder and laughed. "I mean, only days ago, you weren't even a finalist. If memory serves, I think you actually put down the whole thing. I'm sure you didn't even want it . . . not like others might have."

"Like you, you mean?"

She shrugged. "I invested myself in the campaign. I thought it would be fun. My parents came to . . . well, you know."

"So, you think it's unfair that I won?"

"Oh no, DJ, I'm not saying anything like that." Another sugary smile. "Like I said, I think it's very sweet that you won."

She nodded down to DJ's walking cast and cane. "I mean, you *obviously* got the sympathy vote."

DJ pressed her lips together and nodded. "Obviously."

"So, no hard feelings then?" Eliza smiled again. Such a perfect smile. Perfect teeth. Perfect hair and skin. Even perfect words. And yet DJ could never be too sure what lurked beneath the surface.

"No hard feelings from me," said DJ lightly. She grabbed the stair railing with one hand and maneuvered her cane with the other. Then she paused and looked at Eliza. "And your parents are really okay with it too?"

"Other than being a little shocked, they are perfectly fine. Like I already told everyone, they only came up here to show their support for me."

DJ began maneuvering up the stairs. "Well, that's a relief."

"Don't worry, DJ. They're still glad they came up. And, naturally, my mother cannot wait to see me in the fashion show today. Speaking of which, we better get moving."

"Right." DJ grimaced as she took another step.

"Do you need any help?" asked Eliza from behind her.

DJ continued clumping up the stairs. "No, I'm fine." She took in a sharp breath to block the pain shooting through her leg. "Just slow."

"Well, I'm sure you'll be the hit of the fashion show today. Not everyone gets to see a 'crippled' girl going down the runway. *Very sweet*." With that Eliza passed DJ and gracefully jogged up the stairs.

DJ clenched her teeth tighter now. She was determined not to respond to that obvious slam. Really, what was the point? What difference did it make? Still, it was weird how some girls, like Eliza, could knock the wind out of you with just a few sweet-sounding, harmless words and a fake smile. And yet it hurt more than being punched or slapped. Freaky.

"Ready to get beautiful?" asked Taylor as DJ limped into their bedroom.

"Yeah, right." DJ made her way to the bed and dropped her cane as she eased herself down with a long sigh. "Do you really think anyone would miss me if I skipped it?"

"Your grandmother for starters."

"Maybe not ..." DJ actually considered this. "I mean, she's really got her eye on you and Eliza. You guys are the ones with a future in fashion."

"You'd have a future too, DJ. If you wanted it." Taylor kind of laughed. "And if you weren't so handicapped."

"Those are big ifs. But, seriously, my grandmother will be so busy with everything else, she might not even notice my absence."

"Maybe not at first, but eventually she would realize you weren't there, DJ. And, think about it, then she would make you miserable for a few days. Is it really worth it?"

DJ shrugged. "I don't know."

"Come on. Just play along and get it over with."

"Fine. But first I'll take a pain pill and a nap."

"But I thought those pills wiped you out?"

DJ grinned at her. "Will it be my fault if I sleep too late?"

Taylor rolled her eyes as she headed for the bathroom. "It's your funeral."

Carter House Girls Series from Melody Carlson

Mix six teenage girls and one '60s fashion icon (retired, of course) in an old Victorian-era boarding home. Add boys and dating, a little high school angst, and throw in a Kate Spade bag or two ... and you've got the Carter House Girls, Melody Carlson's new chick lit series for young adults!

Mixed Bags
Book One
Softcover • ISBN: 978-0-310-71488-0

Stealing Bradford
Book Two
Softcover • ISBN: 978-0-310-71489-7

Viva Vermont!
Book Four
Softcover • ISBN: 978-0-310-71491-0

Lost in Las Vegas
Book Five
Softcover • ISBN: 978-0-310-71492-7

New York Debut
Book Six
Softcover • ISBN: 978-0-310-71493-4

Books 7–8 coming soon!

Pick up a copy today at your favorite bookstore!

Visit www.zondervan.com/teen

ZONDERVAN®
.com

A Sweet Seasons Novel from Debbie Viguié!

They're fun! They're quirky! They're Sweet Seasons—unlike any other books you've ever read. You could call them alternative, God-honoring chick lit. Join Candy Thompson on a sweet, lighthearted, and honest romp through the friendships, romances, family, school, faith, and values that make a girl's life as full as it can be.

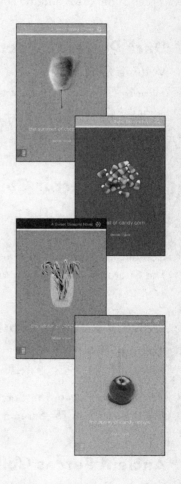

The Summer of Cotton Candy
Book One

Softcover • ISBN: 978-0-310-71558-0

The Fall of Candy Corn
Book Two

Softcover • ISBN: 978-0-310-71559-7

The Winter of Candy Canes
Book Three

Softcover • ISBN: 978-0-310-71752-2

The Spring of Candy Apples
Book Four

Softcover • ISBN: 978-0-310-71753-9

Pick up a copy today at your favorite bookstore!

Visit www.zondervan.com/teen

Forbidden Doors

A Four-Volume Series from Bestselling Author Bill Myers!

Some doors are better left unopened.

Join teenager Rebecca "Becka" Williams, her brother Scott, and her friend Ryan Riordan as they head for mind-bending clashes between the forces of darkness and the kingdom of God.

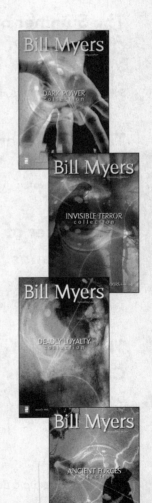

Dark Power Collection
Volume One

Softcover • ISBN: 978-0-310-71534-4

Contains books 1–3: *The Society, The Deceived,* and *The Spell*

Invisible Terror Collection
Volume Two

Softcover • ISBN: 978-0-310-71535-1

Contains books 4–6: *The Haunting, The Guardian,* and *The Encounter*

Deadly Loyalty Collection
Volume Three

Softcover • ISBN: 978-0-310-71536-8

Contains books 7–9: *The Curse, The Undead,* and *The Scream*

Ancient Forces Collection
Volume Four

Softcover • ISBN: 978-0-310-71537-5

Contains books 10–12: *The Ancients, The Wiccan,* and *The Cards*

The Shadowside Trilogy by Robert Elmer!

Those who live in lush comfort on the bright side of the small planet Corista have plundered the water resources of Shadowside for centuries, ignoring the existence of Shadowside's inhabitants, who are nothing more than animals. Or so the Brightsiders have been taught. It will take a special young woman to expose the truth—and to help avert the war that is sure to follow—in the exciting Shadowside Trilogy, the latest sci-fi adventure from Robert Elmer.

Trion Rising
Book One
Softcover • ISBN: 978-0-310-71421-7

The Owling
Book Two
Softcover • ISBN: 978-0-310-71422-4

Beyond Corista
Book Three
Softcover • ISBN: 978-0-310-71423-1

Book 3 coming May 2009!

Pick up a copy today at your favorite bookstore!

Visit www.zondervan.com/teen

The Rayne Tour

by Brandilyn Collins and Amberly Collins!

A suspenseful two-book series for young adults written by bestselling author, Brandilyn Collins, and her daughter, Amberly. The story is about the daughter of a rock star, life on the road, and her search for her real father.

Always Watching
Book One

Softcover • ISBN: 978-0-310-71539-9

This daughter of a rock star has it all—until murder crashes her world. During a concert, sixteen-year-old Shaley O'Connor stumbles upon the body of a friend backstage. Is Tom Hutchens' death connected to her? Frightening messages arrive. Paparazzi stalk Shaley. Her private nightmare is displayed for all to see. Where is God at a time like this? As the clock runs out, Shaley must find Tom's killer—before he strikes again.

Coming May 2009!

Last Breath
Book Two

Softcover • ISBN: 978-0-310-71540-7

With his last breath a dying man whispered four stunning words into Shaley O'Connor's ear. Should she believe them? After two murders on the Rayne concert tour, Shaley is reeling. But she has no time to rest. If the dying man's claim is right, the danger is far from over.

Coming October 2009!

Visit www.zondervan.com/teen

Share Your Thoughts

With the Author: Your comments will be forwarded to the author when you send them to *zauthor@zondervan.com*.

With Zondervan: Submit your review of this book by writing to *zreview@zondervan.com*.

Free Online Resources at
www.zondervan.com

Zondervan AuthorTracker: Be notified whenever your favorite authors publish new books, go on tour, or post an update about what's happening in their lives.

Daily Bible Verses and Devotions: Enrich your life with daily Bible verses or devotions that help you start every morning focused on God.

Free Email Publications: Sign up for newsletters on fiction, Christian living, church ministry, parenting, and more.

Zondervan Bible Search: Find and compare Bible passages in a variety of translations at www.zondervanbiblesearch.com.

Other Benefits: Register yourself to receive online benefits like coupons and special offers, or to participate in research.

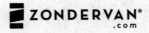